P9-CDD-577

ACCLAIM FOR JEFF SMITH'S

Named an all-time top ten graphic novel by **Time** magazine.

"As sweeping as the 'Lord of the Rings' cycle, but much funnier."　　　　　—Andrew Arnold, **Time.com**

★"This is first-class kid lit: exciting, funny, scary, and resonant enough that it will stick with readers for a long time."　　　—**Publishers Weekly,** starred review

PRAISE FOR ROSE

"ROSE is a magnificent prequel to Jeff Smith's **BONE.**"
　　　　　—Neil Gaiman, author of **Coraline**

"I love Charles Vess' art so much that I'll buy anything he illustrates, but his collaboration with Jeff Smith on ROSE has really upped the ante."
　　　—Charles de Lint, award-winning fantasy writer

THE ***BONE*** SAGA

Out from Boneville

The Great Cow Race

Eyes of the Storm

The Dragonslayer

Rock Jaw: Master of the Eastern Border

Old Man's Cave

Ghost Circles

Treasure Hunters

Crown of Horns

ROSE

BY JEFF SMITH

WITH ILLUSTRATIONS BY
CHARLES VESS

An Imprint of
■SCHOLASTIC

New York   Toronto   London   Auckland   Sydney   Mexico City   New Delhi   Hong Kong   Buenos Aires

This book is dedicated to Karen and Vijaya

Copyright © 2009 by Jeff Smith.

The chapters in this book were originally published in the comic book *ROSE* and are copyright
© 2000, 2001, and 2002 by Jeff Smith. *ROSE*™ is © 2009 by Jeff Smith.

All rights reserved. Published by Graphix, an imprint of Scholastic Inc., *Publishers since 1920.*
SCHOLASTIC, GRAPHIX, and associated logos are trademarks and/or registered trademarks of
Scholastic Inc.

No part of this publication may be reproduced, stored in a retrieval system, or transmitted in any
form or by any means, electronic, mechanical, photocopying, recording, or otherwise, without
written permission of the publisher. For information regarding permission, write to Scholastic Inc.,
Attention: Permissions Department, 557 Broadway, New York, NY 10012.

Library of Congress Catalog Card Number 9568403.
ISBN-13 978-0-545-13542-9 — ISBN-10 0-545-13542-7
ISBN 0-545-13543-5 (paperback)

ACKNOWLEDGMENTS
Harvestar Family Crest designed by Charles Vess
Map of *The Valley* by Mark Crilley
Illustration and font design by Charles Vess

10 9 8 7 6 5 4 3 2 1   09 10 11 12
First Scholastic edition, August 2009
Book design by David Saylor
Printed in Singapore 46

CONTENTS

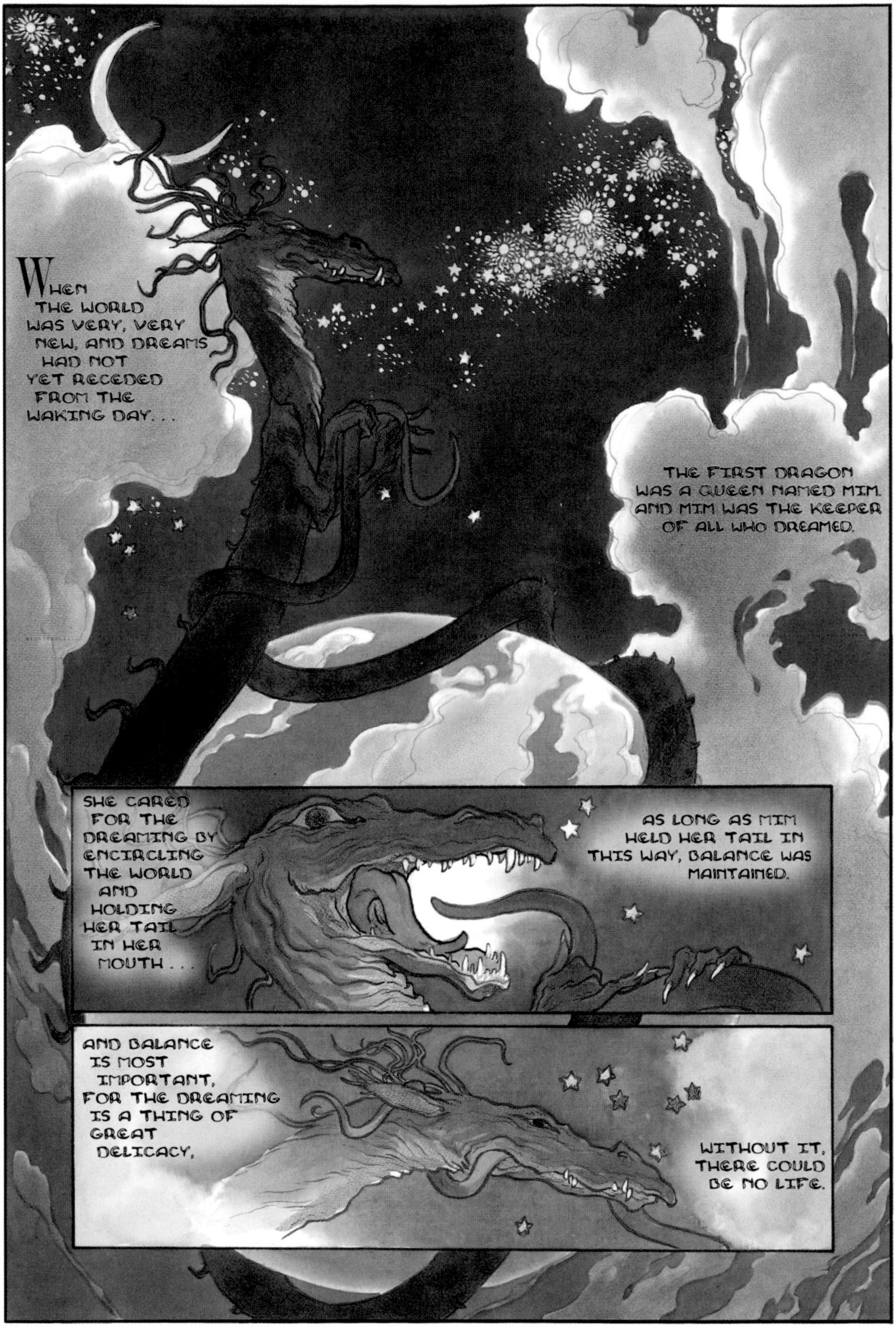
WHEN THE WORLD WAS VERY, VERY NEW, AND DREAMS HAD NOT YET RECEDED FROM THE WAKING DAY. . .
THE FIRST DRAGON WAS A QUEEN NAMED MIM. AND MIM WAS THE KEEPER OF ALL WHO DREAMED.
SHE CARED FOR THE DREAMING BY ENCIRCLING THE WORLD AND HOLDING HER TAIL IN HER MOUTH . . .
AS LONG AS MIM HELD HER TAIL IN THIS WAY, BALANCE WAS MAINTAINED.
AND BALANCE IS MOST IMPORTANT, FOR THE DREAMING IS A THING OF GREAT DELICACY,
WITHOUT IT, THERE COULD BE NO LIFE.

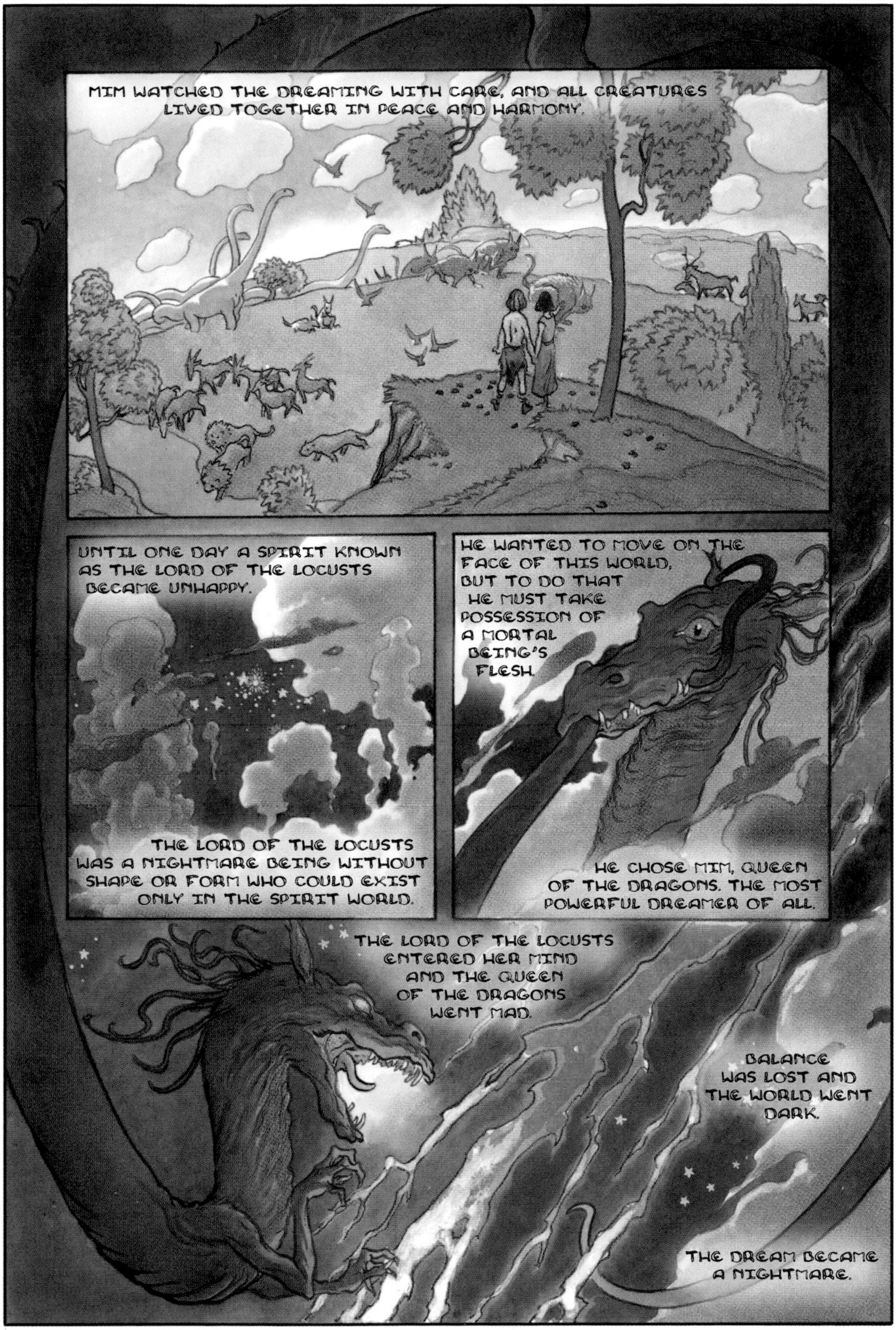
MIM WATCHED THE DREAMING WITH CARE, AND ALL CREATURES LIVED TOGETHER IN PEACE AND HARMONY.
UNTIL ONE DAY A SPIRIT KNOWN AS THE LORD OF THE LOCUSTS BECAME UNHAPPY.
THE LORD OF THE LOCUSTS WAS A NIGHTMARE BEING WITHOUT SHAPE OR FORM WHO COULD EXIST ONLY IN THE SPIRIT WORLD.
HE WANTED TO MOVE ON THE FACE OF THIS WORLD, BUT TO DO THAT HE MUST TAKE POSSESSION OF A MORTAL BEING'S FLESH.
HE CHOSE MIM, QUEEN OF THE DRAGONS. THE MOST POWERFUL DREAMER OF ALL.
THE LORD OF THE LOCUSTS ENTERED HER MIND AND THE QUEEN OF THE DRAGONS WENT MAD.
BALANCE WAS LOST AND THE WORLD WENT DARK.
THE DREAM BECAME A NIGHTMARE.

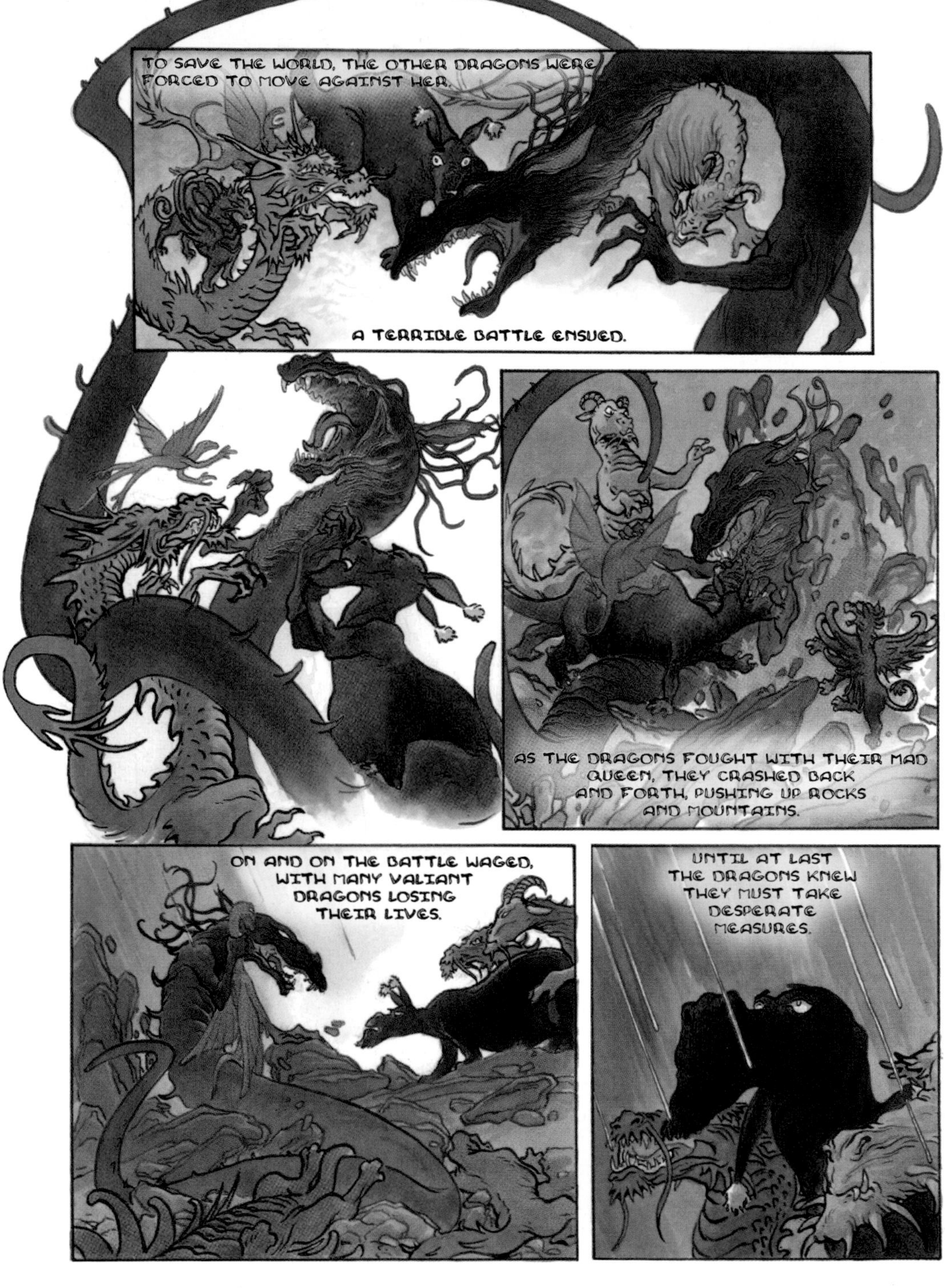
TO SAVE THE WORLD, THE OTHER DRAGONS WERE FORCED TO MOVE AGAINST HER.
A TERRIBLE BATTLE ENSUED.
AS THE DRAGONS FOUGHT WITH THEIR MAD QUEEN, THEY CRASHED BACK AND FORTH, PUSHING UP ROCKS AND MOUNTAINS.
ON AND ON THE BATTLE WAGED, WITH MANY VALIANT DRAGONS LOSING THEIR LIVES.
UNTIL AT LAST THE DRAGONS KNEW THEY MUST TAKE DESPERATE MEASURES.

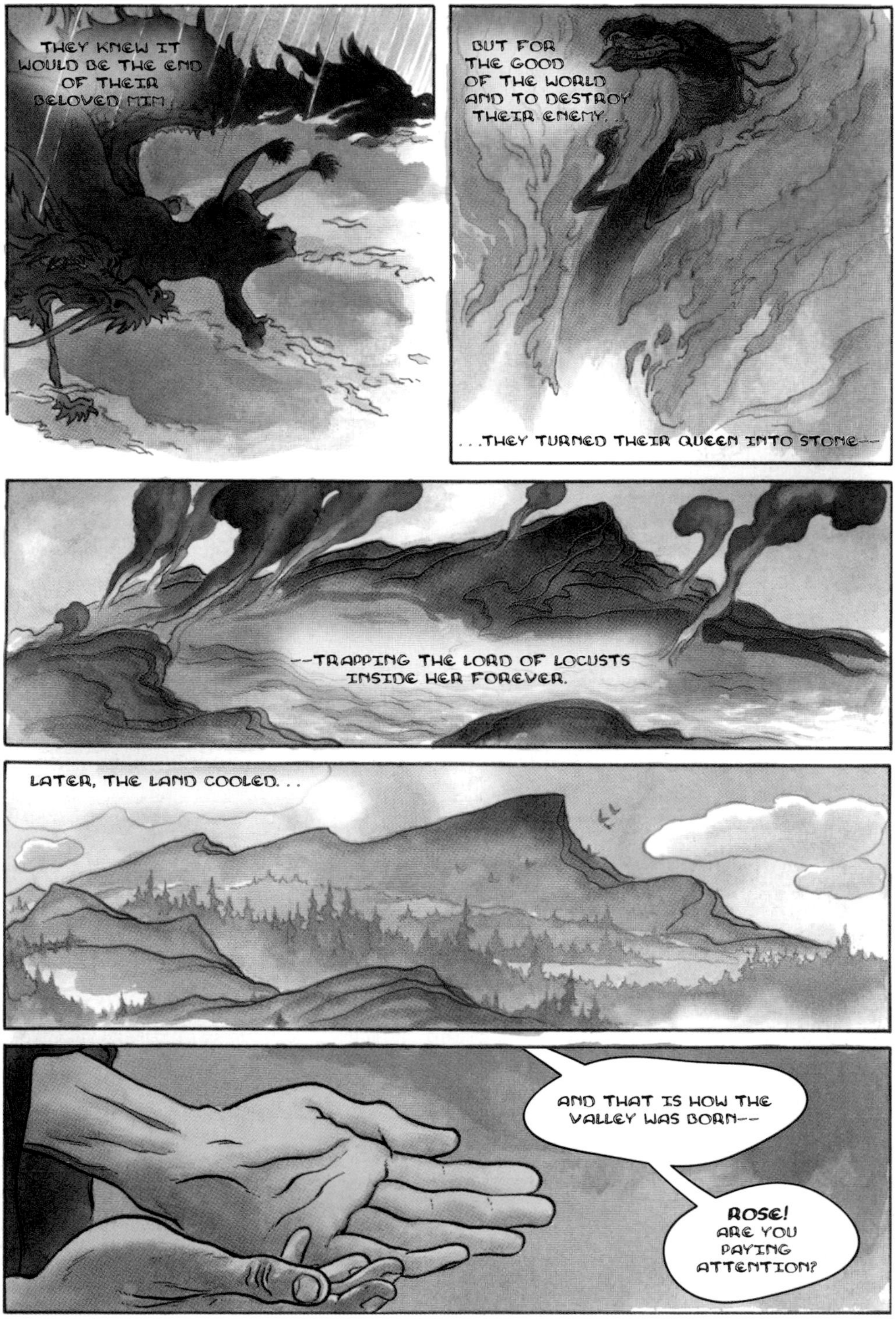
THEY KNEW IT WOULD BE THE END OF THEIR BELOVED MIM . . .
BUT FOR THE GOOD OF THE WORLD AND TO DESTROY THEIR ENEMY. . .
. . .THEY TURNED THEIR QUEEN INTO STONE--
--TRAPPING THE LORD OF LOCUSTS INSIDE HER FOREVER.
LATER, THE LAND COOLED. . .
AND THAT IS HOW THE VALLEY WAS BORN--
ROSE! ARE YOU PAYING ATTENTION?

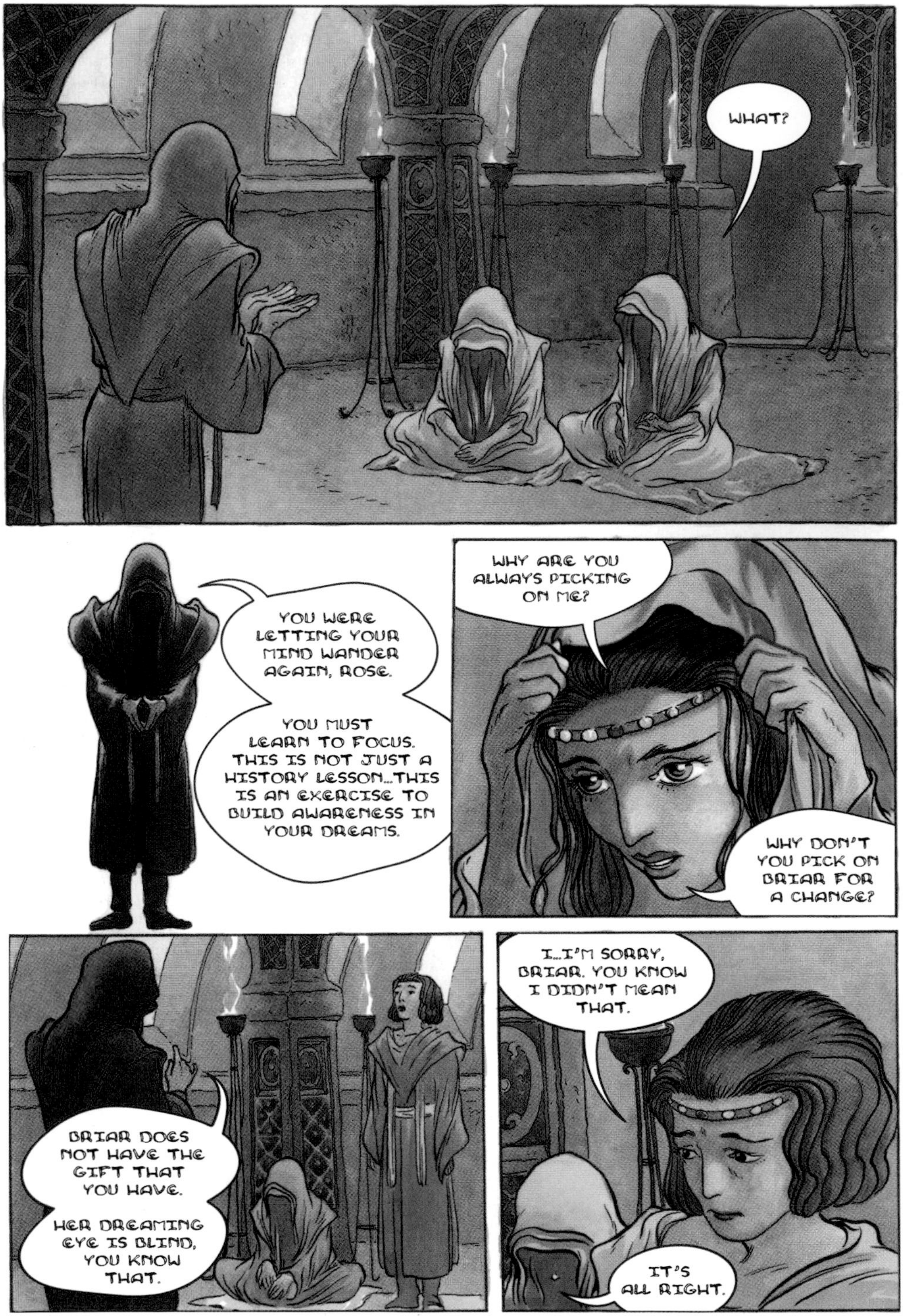
WHAT?
YOU WERE LETTING YOUR MIND WANDER AGAIN, ROSE.
YOU MUST LEARN TO FOCUS. THIS IS NOT JUST A HISTORY LESSON...THIS IS AN EXERCISE TO BUILD AWARENESS IN YOUR DREAMS.
WHY ARE YOU ALWAYS PICKING ON ME?
WHY DON'T YOU PICK ON BRIAR FOR A CHANGE?
BRIAR DOES NOT HAVE THE GIFT THAT YOU HAVE.
HER DREAMING EYE IS BLIND, YOU KNOW THAT.
I...I'M SORRY, BRIAR. YOU KNOW I DIDN'T MEAN THAT.
IT'S ALL RIGHT.

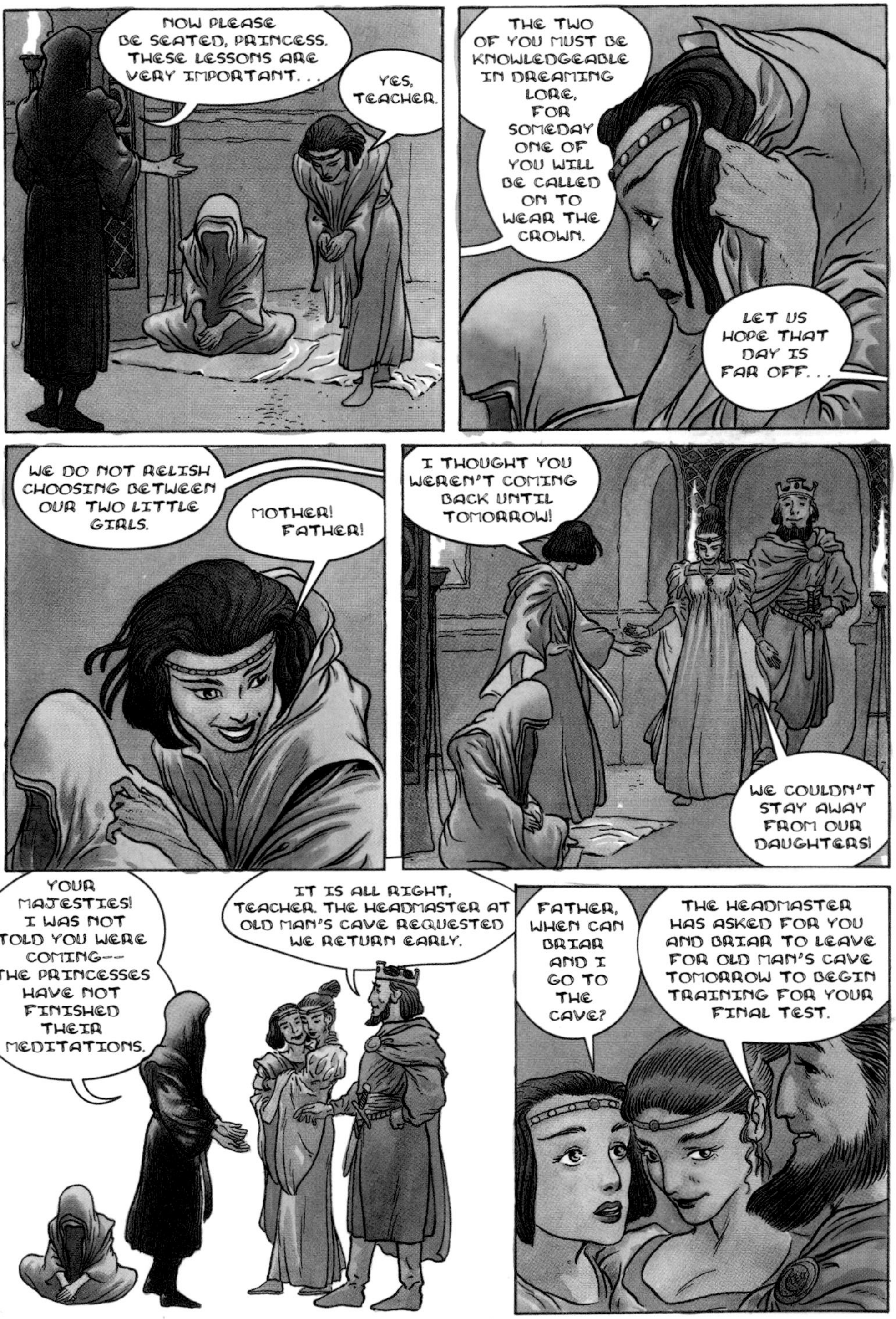
NOW PLEASE BE SEATED, PRINCESS. THESE LESSONS ARE VERY IMPORTANT...
YES, TEACHER.
THE TWO OF YOU MUST BE KNOWLEDGEABLE IN DREAMING LORE, FOR SOMEDAY ONE OF YOU WILL BE CALLED ON TO WEAR THE CROWN.
LET US HOPE THAT DAY IS FAR OFF...
WE DO NOT RELISH CHOOSING BETWEEN OUR TWO LITTLE GIRLS.
MOTHER! FATHER!
I THOUGHT YOU WEREN'T COMING BACK UNTIL TOMORROW!
WE COULDN'T STAY AWAY FROM OUR DAUGHTERS!
YOUR MAJESTIES! I WAS NOT TOLD YOU WERE COMING-- THE PRINCESSES HAVE NOT FINISHED THEIR MEDITATIONS.
IT IS ALL RIGHT, TEACHER. THE HEADMASTER AT OLD MAN'S CAVE REQUESTED WE RETURN EARLY.
FATHER, WHEN CAN BRIAR AND I GO TO THE CAVE?
THE HEADMASTER HAS ASKED FOR YOU AND BRIAR TO LEAVE FOR OLD MAN'S CAVE TOMORROW TO BEGIN TRAINING FOR YOUR FINAL TEST.

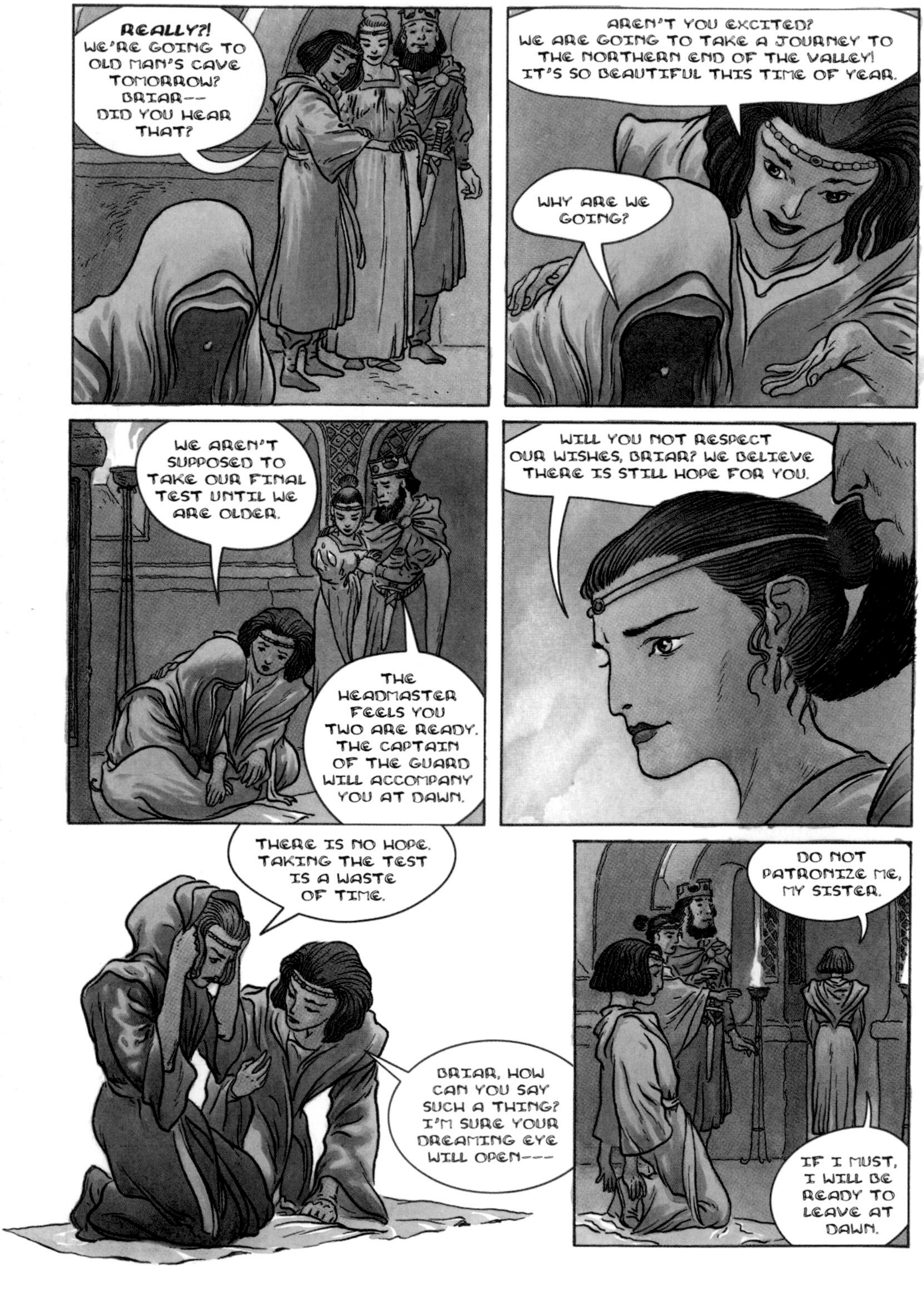
REALLY?!
WE'RE GOING TO OLD MAN'S CAVE TOMORROW? BRIAR-- DID YOU HEAR THAT?
AREN'T YOU EXCITED? WE ARE GOING TO TAKE A JOURNEY TO THE NORTHERN END OF THE VALLEY! IT'S SO BEAUTIFUL THIS TIME OF YEAR.
WHY ARE WE GOING?
WE AREN'T SUPPOSED TO TAKE OUR FINAL TEST UNTIL WE ARE OLDER.
THE HEADMASTER FEELS YOU TWO ARE READY. THE CAPTAIN OF THE GUARD WILL ACCOMPANY YOU AT DAWN.
WILL YOU NOT RESPECT OUR WISHES, BRIAR? WE BELIEVE THERE IS STILL HOPE FOR YOU.
THERE IS NO HOPE. TAKING THE TEST IS A WASTE OF TIME.
BRIAR, HOW CAN YOU SAY SUCH A THING? I'M SURE YOUR DREAMING EYE WILL OPEN---
DO NOT PATRONIZE ME, MY SISTER.
IF I MUST, I WILL BE READY TO LEAVE AT DAWN.

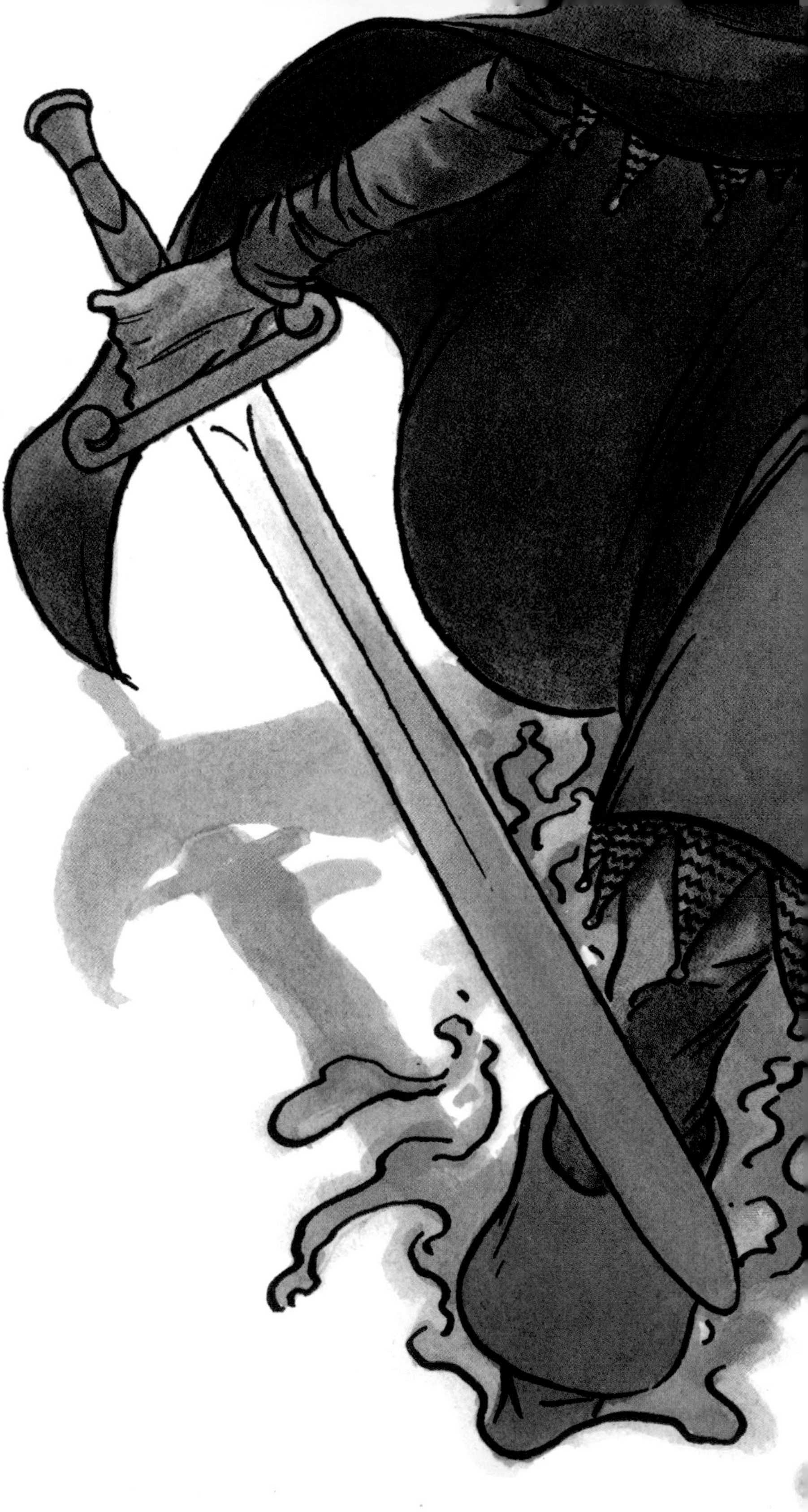

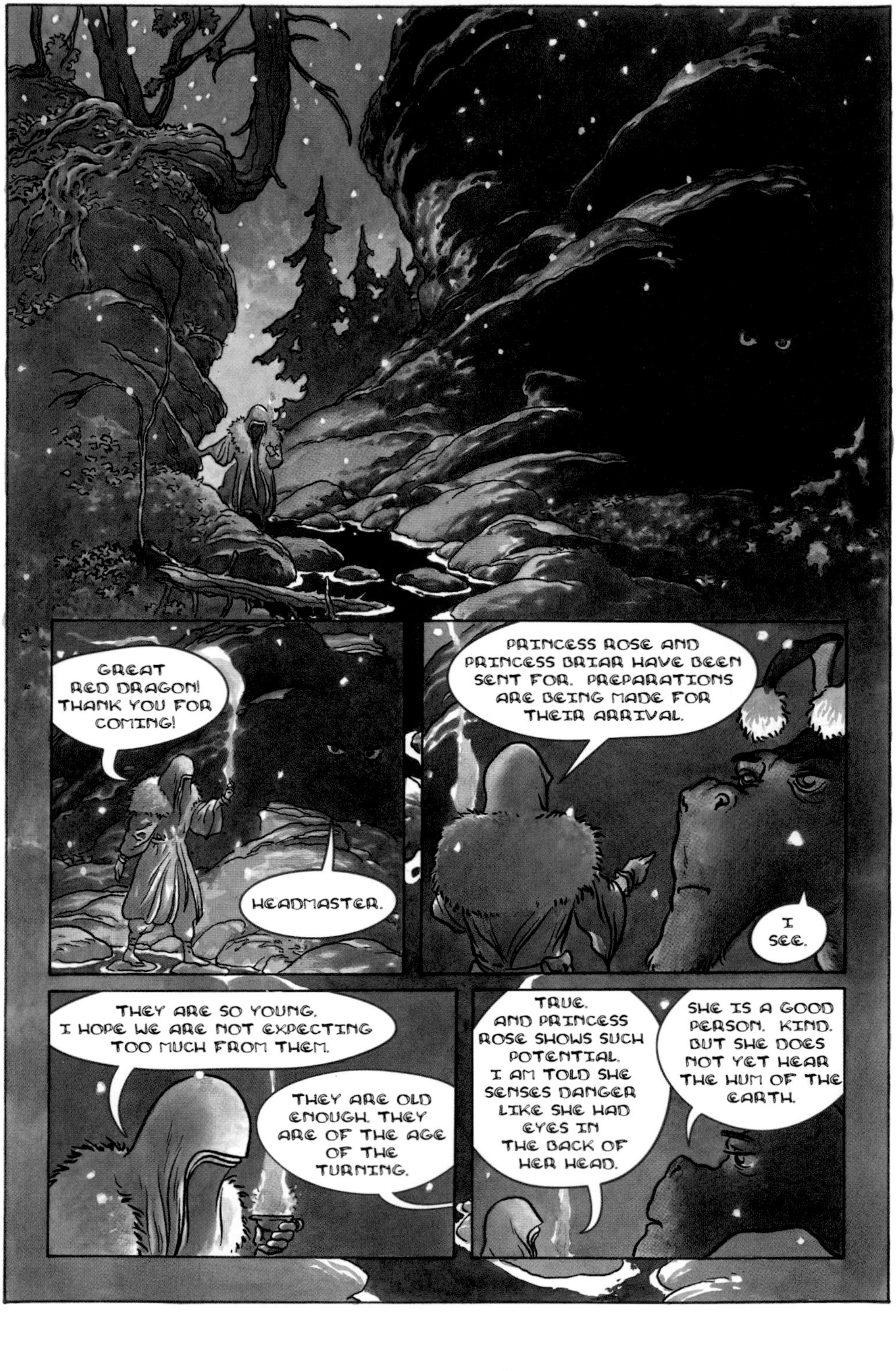
GREAT RED DRAGON! THANK YOU FOR COMING!
HEADMASTER.
PRINCESS ROSE AND PRINCESS BRIAR HAVE BEEN SENT FOR. PREPARATIONS ARE BEING MADE FOR THEIR ARRIVAL.
I SEE.
THEY ARE SO YOUNG. I HOPE WE ARE NOT EXPECTING TOO MUCH FROM THEM.
THEY ARE OLD ENOUGH. THEY ARE OF THE AGE OF THE TURNING.
TRUE. AND PRINCESS ROSE SHOWS SUCH POTENTIAL. I AM TOLD SHE SENSES DANGER LIKE SHE HAD EYES IN THE BACK OF HER HEAD.
SHE IS A GOOD PERSON. KIND. BUT SHE DOES NOT YET HEAR THE HUM OF THE EARTH.

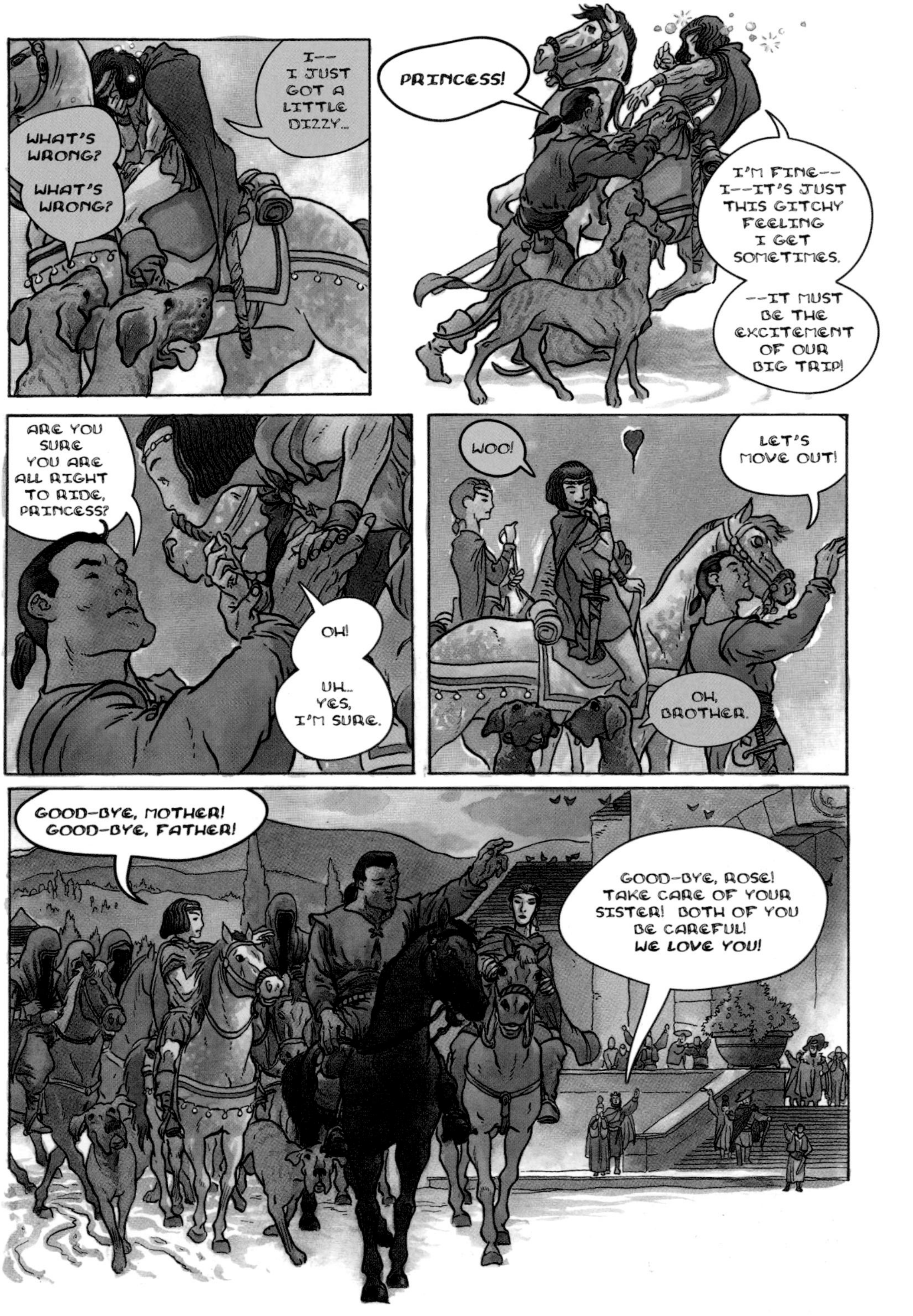
I-- I JUST GOT A LITTLE DIZZY...
WHAT'S WRONG?
WHAT'S WRONG?
PRINCESS!
I'M FINE-- I--IT'S JUST THIS GITCHY FEELING I GET SOMETIMES.
--IT MUST BE THE EXCITEMENT OF OUR BIG TRIP!
ARE YOU SURE YOU ARE ALL RIGHT TO RIDE, PRINCESS?
OH!
UH... YES, I'M SURE.
WOO!
LET'S MOVE OUT!
OH, BROTHER.
GOOD-BYE, MOTHER! GOOD-BYE, FATHER!
GOOD-BYE, ROSE! TAKE CARE OF YOUR SISTER! BOTH OF YOU BE CAREFUL! WE LOVE YOU!

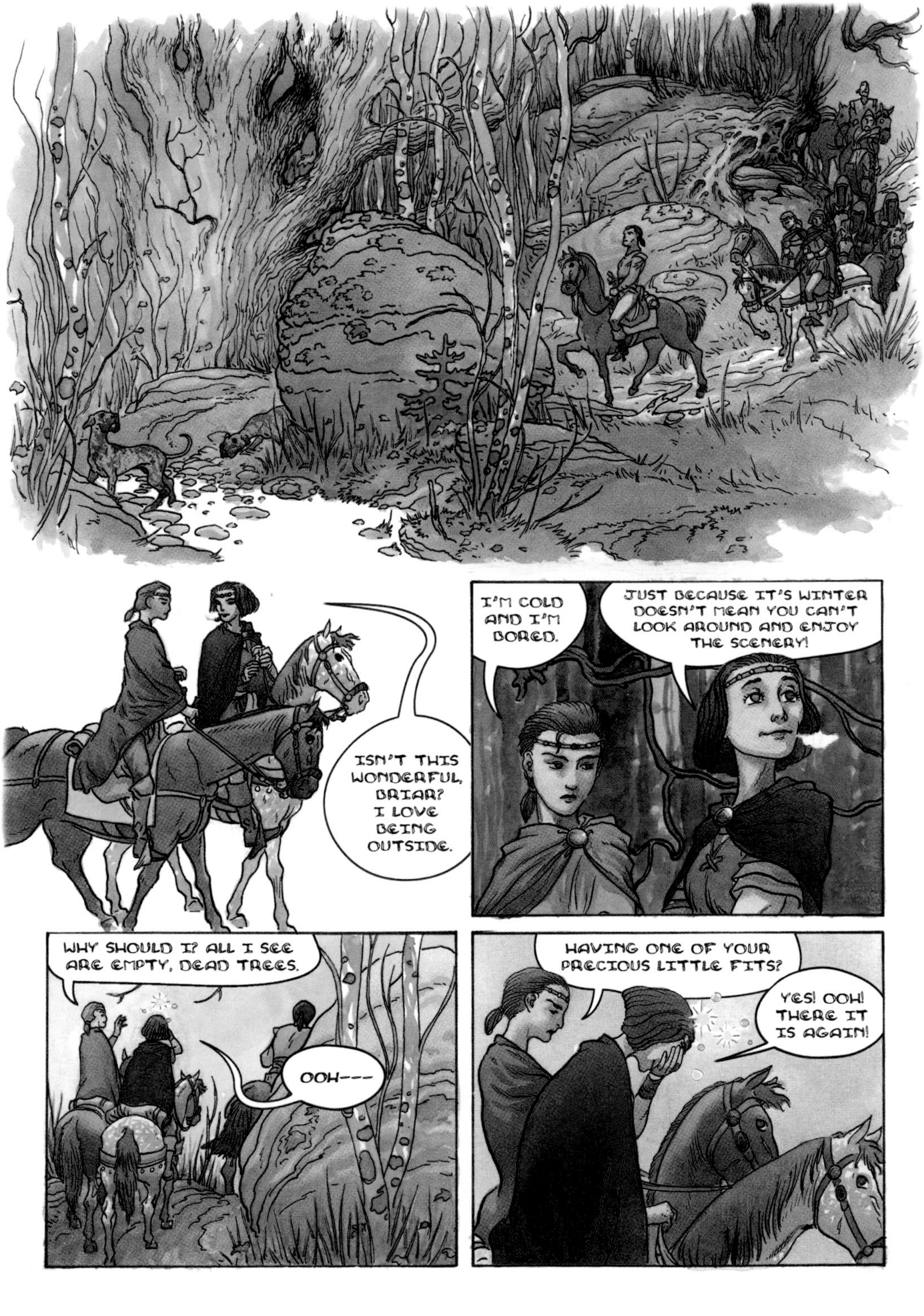
ISN'T THIS WONDERFUL, BRIAR? I LOVE BEING OUTSIDE.
I'M COLD AND I'M BORED.
JUST BECAUSE IT'S WINTER DOESN'T MEAN YOU CAN'T LOOK AROUND AND ENJOY THE SCENERY!
WHY SHOULD I? ALL I SEE ARE EMPTY, DEAD TREES.
OOH---
HAVING ONE OF YOUR PRECIOUS LITTLE FITS?
YES! OOH! THERE IT IS AGAIN!

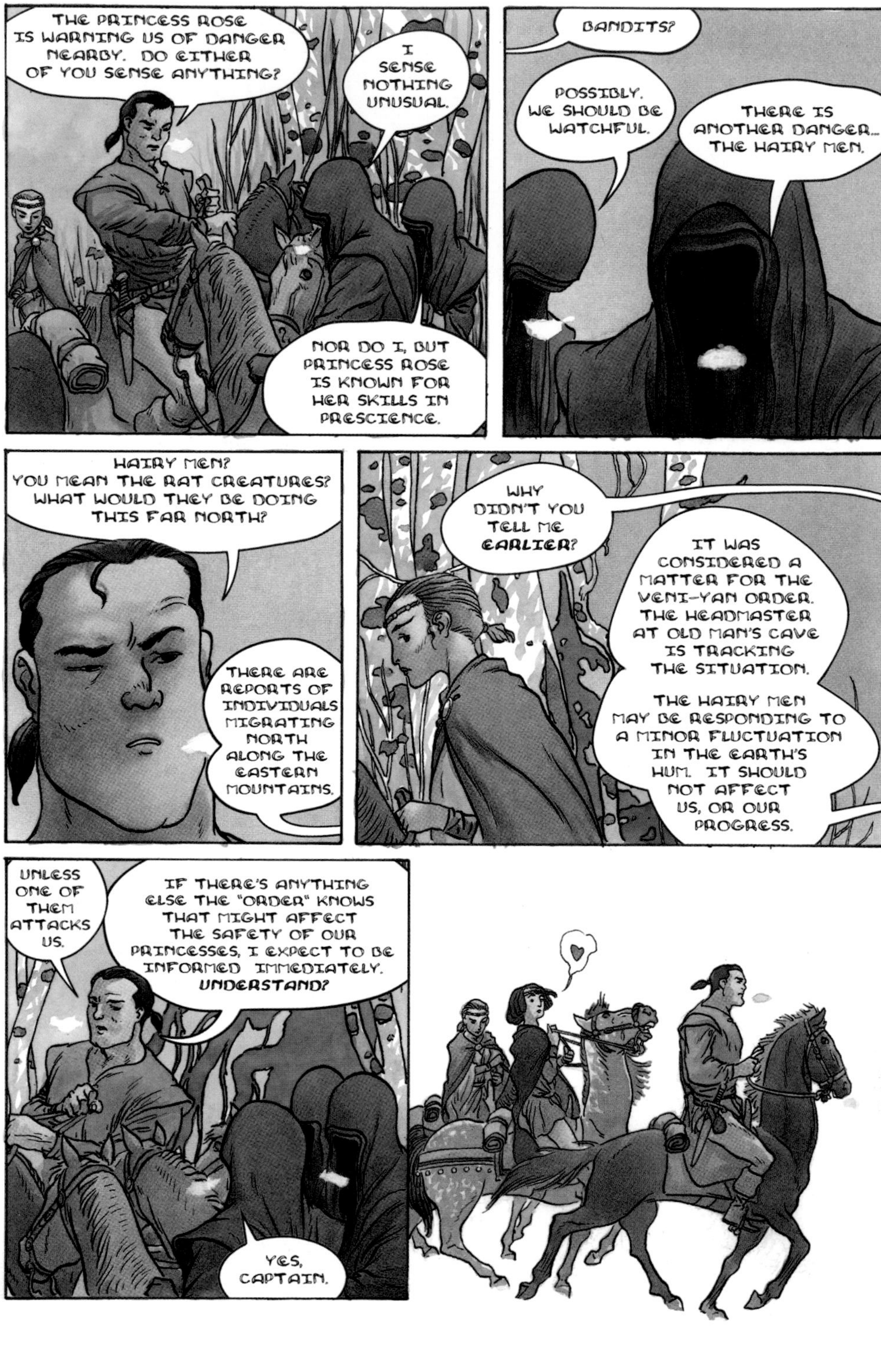
THE PRINCESS ROSE IS WARNING US OF DANGER NEARBY. DO EITHER OF YOU SENSE ANYTHING?
I SENSE NOTHING UNUSUAL.
NOR DO I, BUT PRINCESS ROSE IS KNOWN FOR HER SKILLS IN PRESCIENCE.
BANDITS?
POSSIBLY. WE SHOULD BE WATCHFUL.
THERE IS ANOTHER DANGER... THE HAIRY MEN.
HAIRY MEN? YOU MEAN THE RAT CREATURES? WHAT WOULD THEY BE DOING THIS FAR NORTH?
THERE ARE REPORTS OF INDIVIDUALS MIGRATING NORTH ALONG THE EASTERN MOUNTAINS.
WHY DIDN'T YOU TELL ME EARLIER?
IT WAS CONSIDERED A MATTER FOR THE VENI-YAN ORDER. THE HEADMASTER AT OLD MAN'S CAVE IS TRACKING THE SITUATION.
THE HAIRY MEN MAY BE RESPONDING TO A MINOR FLUCTUATION IN THE EARTH'S HUM. IT SHOULD NOT AFFECT US, OR OUR PROGRESS.
UNLESS ONE OF THEM ATTACKS US.
IF THERE'S ANYTHING ELSE THE "ORDER" KNOWS THAT MIGHT AFFECT THE SAFETY OF OUR PRINCESSES, I EXPECT TO BE INFORMED IMMEDIATELY. UNDERSTAND?
YES, CAPTAIN.

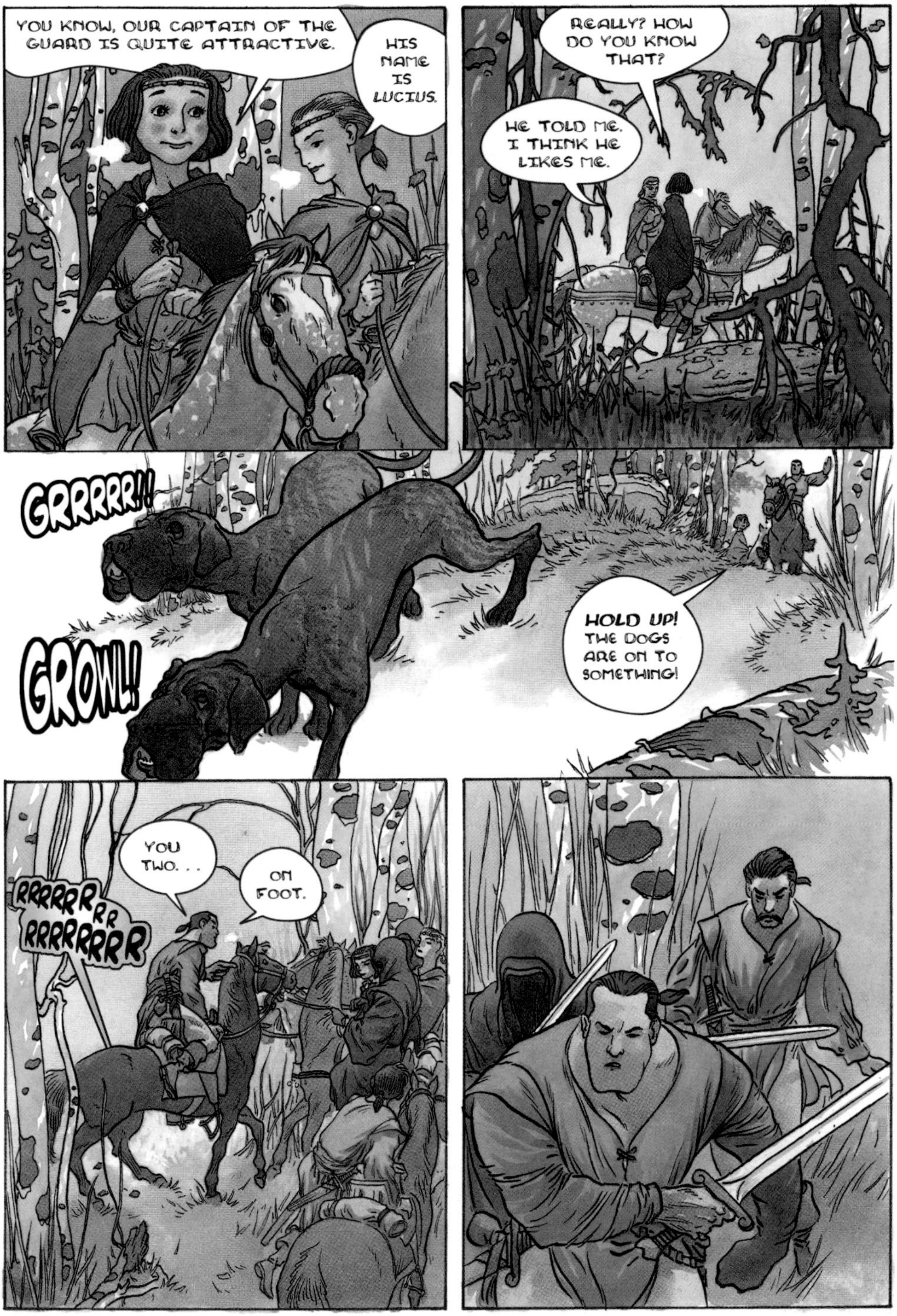
YOU KNOW, OUR CAPTAIN OF THE GUARD IS QUITE ATTRACTIVE.
HIS NAME IS *LUCIUS.*
REALLY? HOW DO YOU KNOW THAT?
HE TOLD ME. I THINK HE LIKES ME.
GRRRRR!!
GROWL!
HOLD UP! THE DOGS ARE ON TO SOMETHING!
YOU TWO. . .
ON FOOT.
RRRRRRRR RRRRRRRR

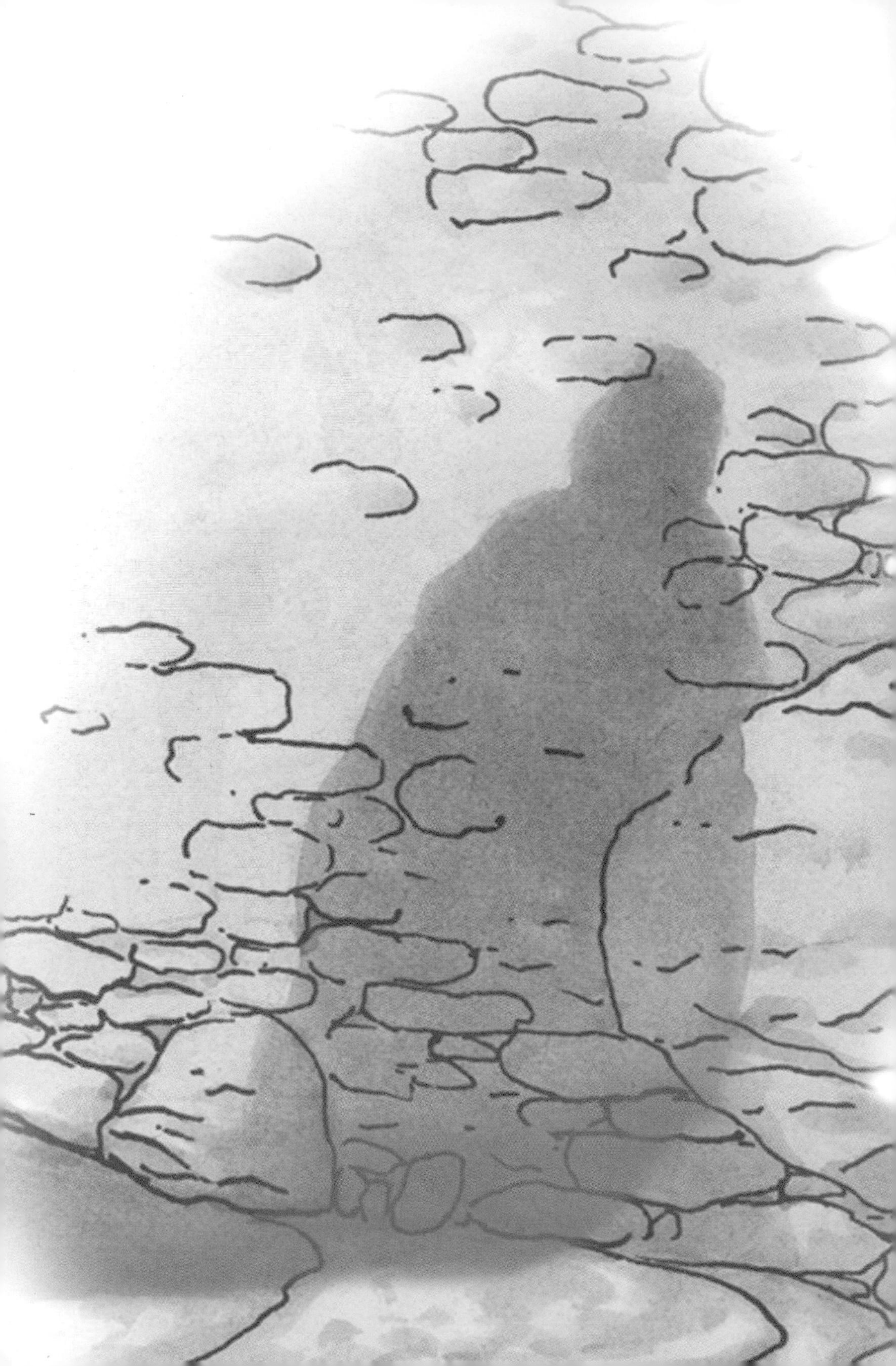

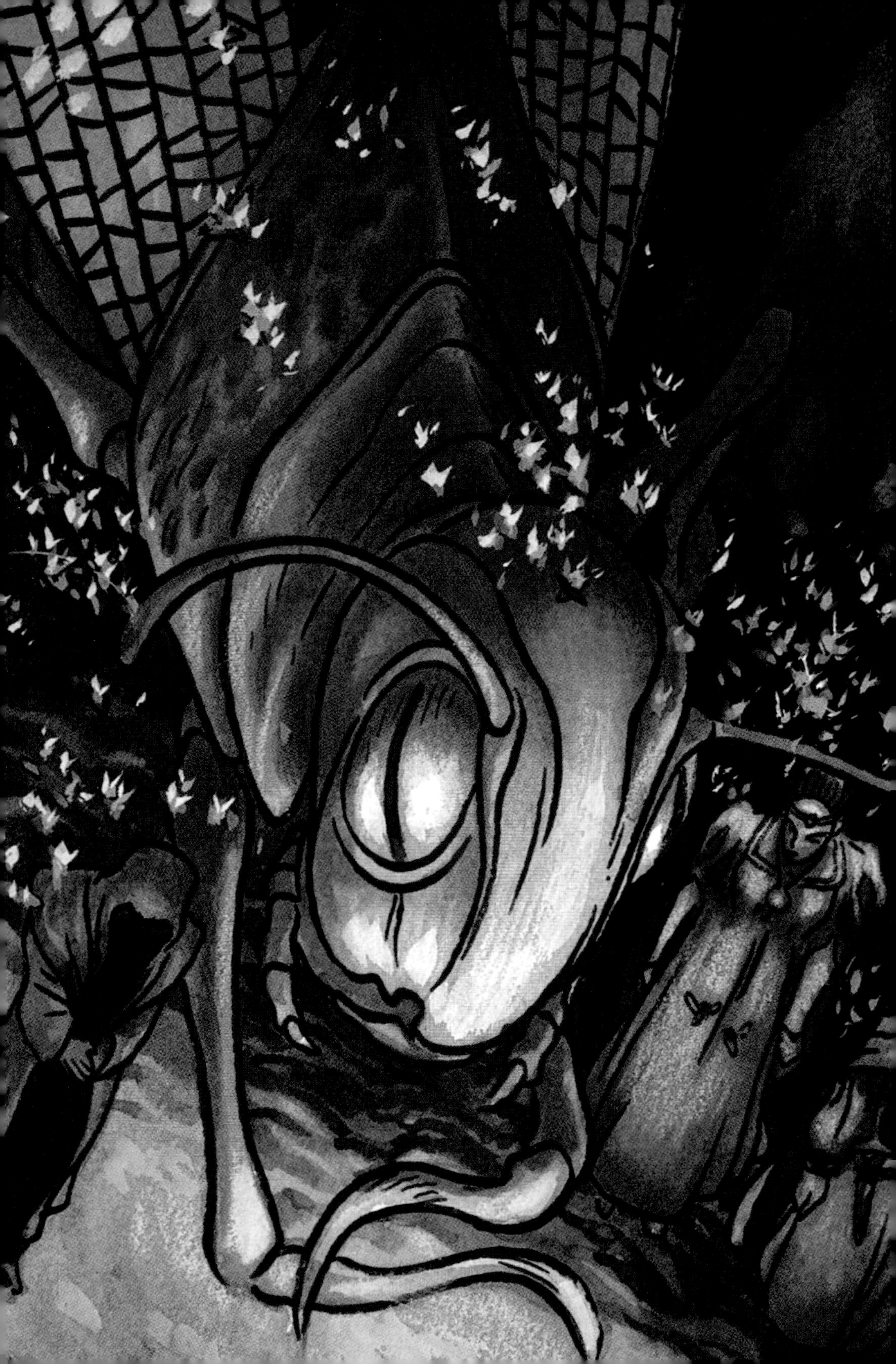

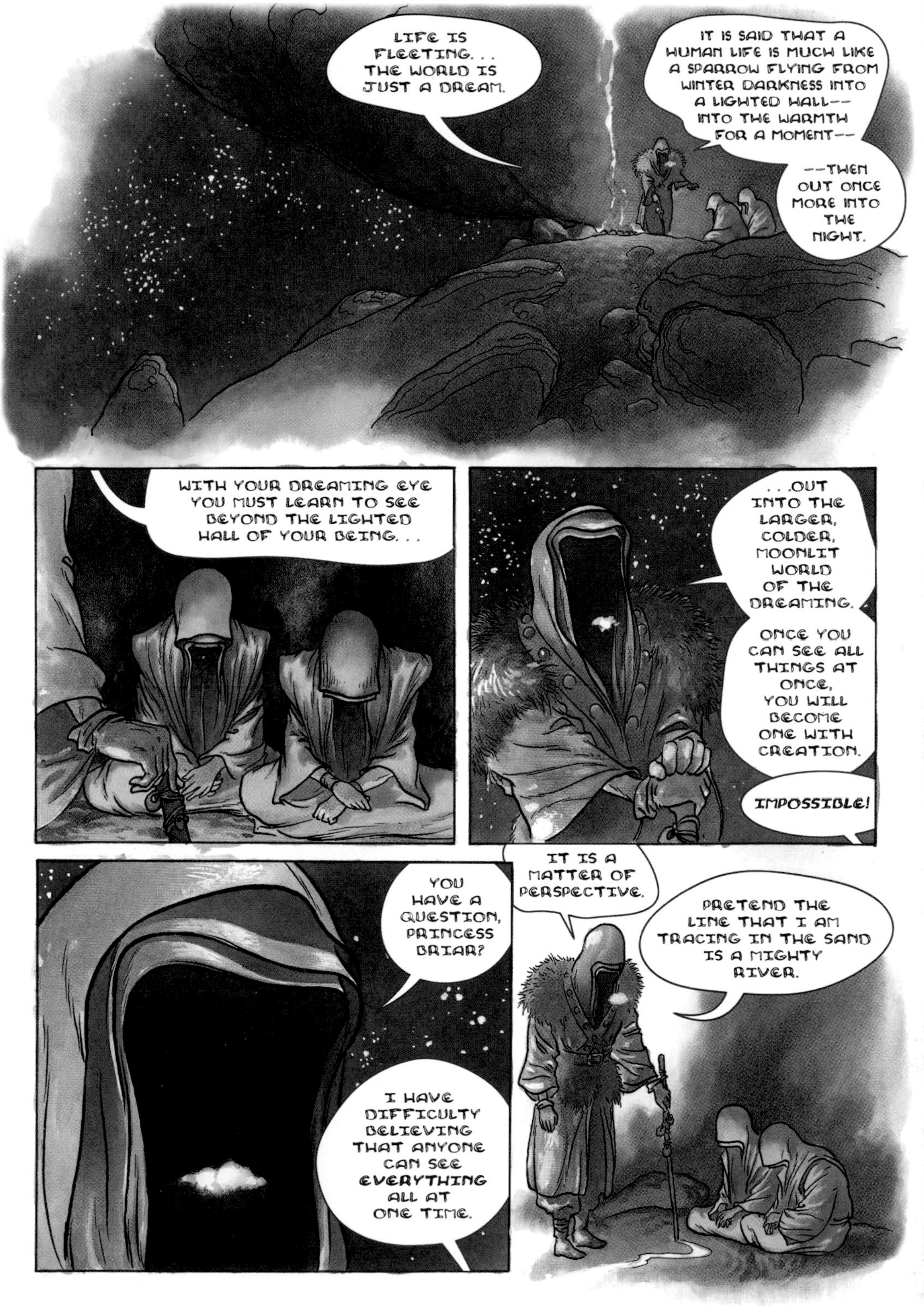
LIFE IS FLEETING. . . THE WORLD IS JUST A DREAM.
IT IS SAID THAT A HUMAN LIFE IS MUCH LIKE A SPARROW FLYING FROM WINTER DARKNESS INTO A LIGHTED HALL-- INTO THE WARMTH FOR A MOMENT--
--THEN OUT ONCE MORE INTO THE NIGHT.
WITH YOUR DREAMING EYE YOU MUST LEARN TO SEE BEYOND THE LIGHTED HALL OF YOUR BEING. . .
. . .OUT INTO THE LARGER, COLDER, MOONLIT WORLD OF THE DREAMING.
ONCE YOU CAN SEE ALL THINGS AT ONCE, YOU WILL BECOME ONE WITH CREATION.
IMPOSSIBLE!
YOU HAVE A QUESTION, PRINCESS BRIAR?
I HAVE DIFFICULTY BELIEVING THAT ANYONE CAN SEE EVERYTHING ALL AT ONE TIME.
IT IS A MATTER OF PERSPECTIVE.
PRETEND THE LINE THAT I AM TRACING IN THE SAND IS A MIGHTY RIVER.

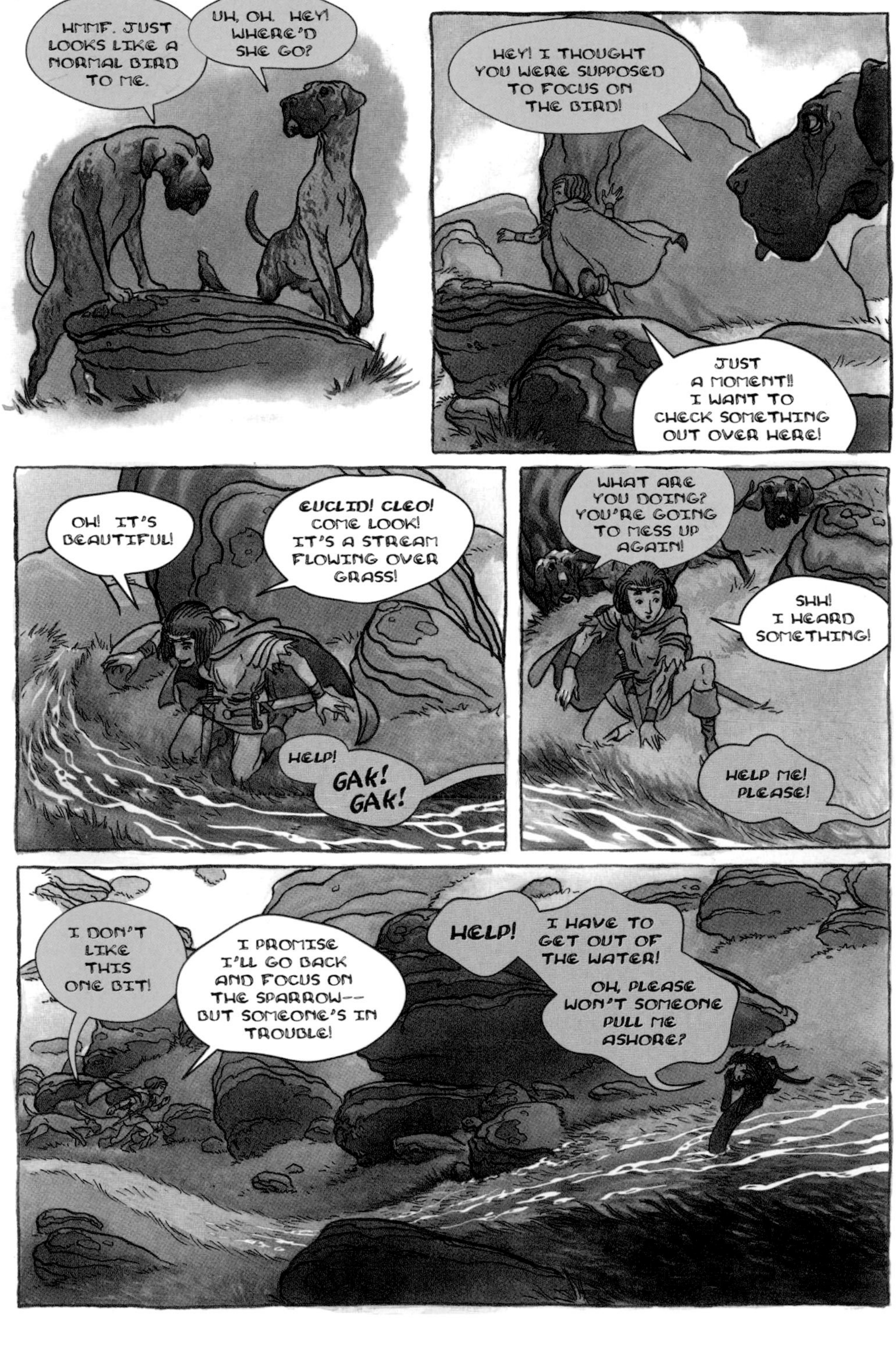
HMMF. JUST LOOKS LIKE A NORMAL BIRD TO ME.
UH, OH. HEY! WHERE'D SHE GO?
HEY! I THOUGHT YOU WERE SUPPOSED TO FOCUS ON THE BIRD!
JUST A MOMENT!! I WANT TO CHECK SOMETHING OUT OVER HERE!
OH! IT'S BEAUTIFUL!
EUCLID! CLEO! COME LOOK! IT'S A STREAM FLOWING OVER GRASS!
HELP!
GAK! GAK!
WHAT ARE YOU DOING? YOU'RE GOING TO MESS UP AGAIN!
SHH! I HEARD SOMETHING!
HELP ME! PLEASE!
I DON'T LIKE THIS ONE BIT!
I PROMISE I'LL GO BACK AND FOCUS ON THE SPARROW-- BUT SOMEONE'S IN TROUBLE!
HELP!
I HAVE TO GET OUT OF THE WATER!
OH, PLEASE WON'T SOMEONE PULL ME ASHORE?

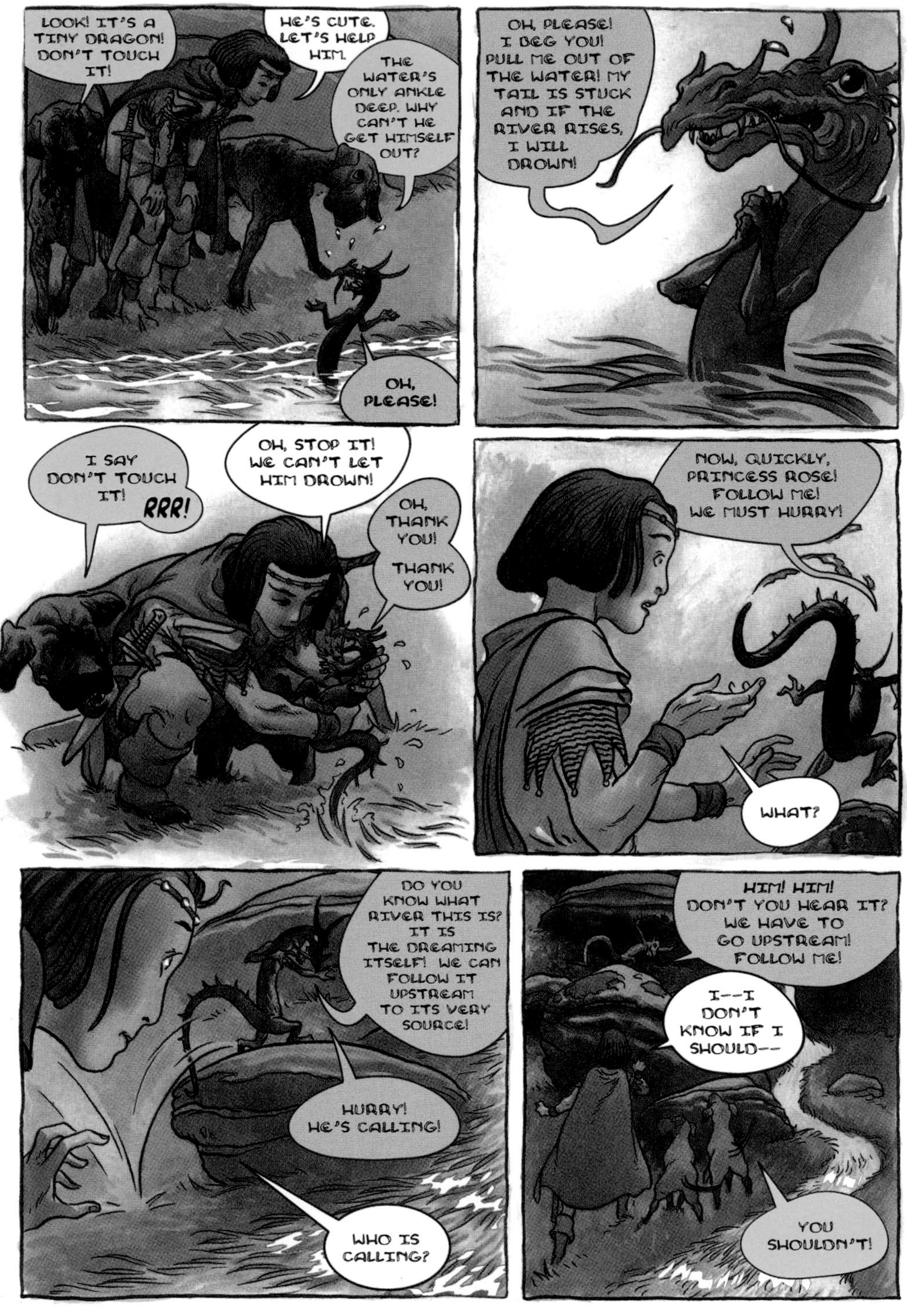
LOOK! IT'S A TINY DRAGON! DON'T TOUCH IT!
HE'S CUTE. LET'S HELP HIM.
THE WATER'S ONLY ANKLE DEEP. WHY CAN'T HE GET HIMSELF OUT?
OH, PLEASE!
OH, PLEASE! I BEG YOU! PULL ME OUT OF THE WATER! MY TAIL IS STUCK AND IF THE RIVER RISES, I WILL DROWN!
I SAY DON'T TOUCH IT! RRR!
OH, STOP IT! WE CAN'T LET HIM DROWN!
OH, THANK YOU!
THANK YOU!
NOW, QUICKLY, PRINCESS ROSE! FOLLOW ME! WE MUST HURRY!
WHAT?
DO YOU KNOW WHAT RIVER THIS IS? IT IS THE DREAMING ITSELF! WE CAN FOLLOW IT UPSTREAM TO ITS VERY SOURCE!
HURRY! HE'S CALLING!
WHO IS CALLING?
HIM! HIM! DON'T YOU HEAR IT? WE HAVE TO GO UPSTREAM! FOLLOW ME!
I--I DON'T KNOW IF I SHOULD--
YOU SHOULDN'T!

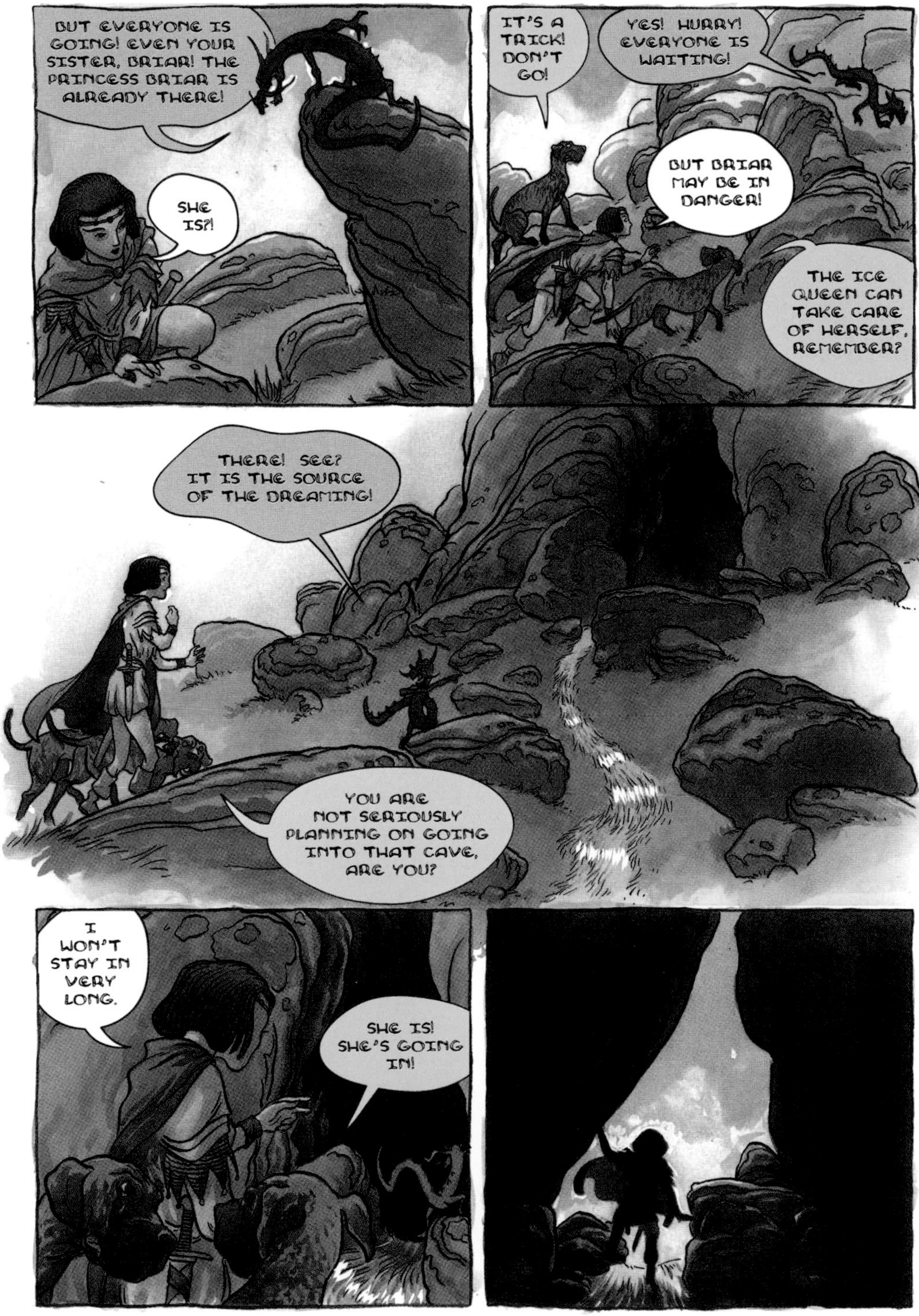
BUT EVERYONE IS GOING! EVEN YOUR SISTER, BRIAR! THE PRINCESS BRIAR IS ALREADY THERE!
SHE IS?!
IT'S A TRICK! DON'T GO!
YES! HURRY! EVERYONE IS WAITING!
BUT BRIAR MAY BE IN DANGER!
THE ICE QUEEN CAN TAKE CARE OF HERSELF, REMEMBER?
THERE! SEE? IT IS THE SOURCE OF THE DREAMING!
YOU ARE NOT SERIOUSLY PLANNING ON GOING INTO THAT CAVE, ARE YOU?
I WON'T STAY IN VERY LONG.
SHE IS! SHE'S GOING IN!

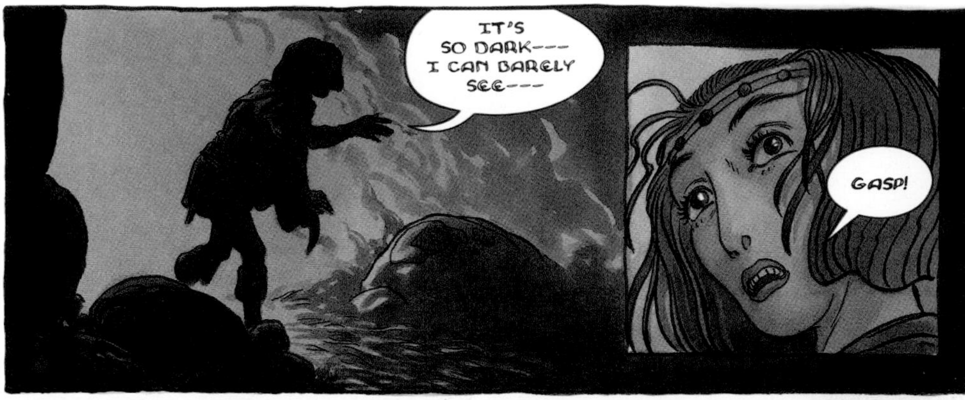
IT'S SO DARK--- I CAN BARELY SEE---
GASP!

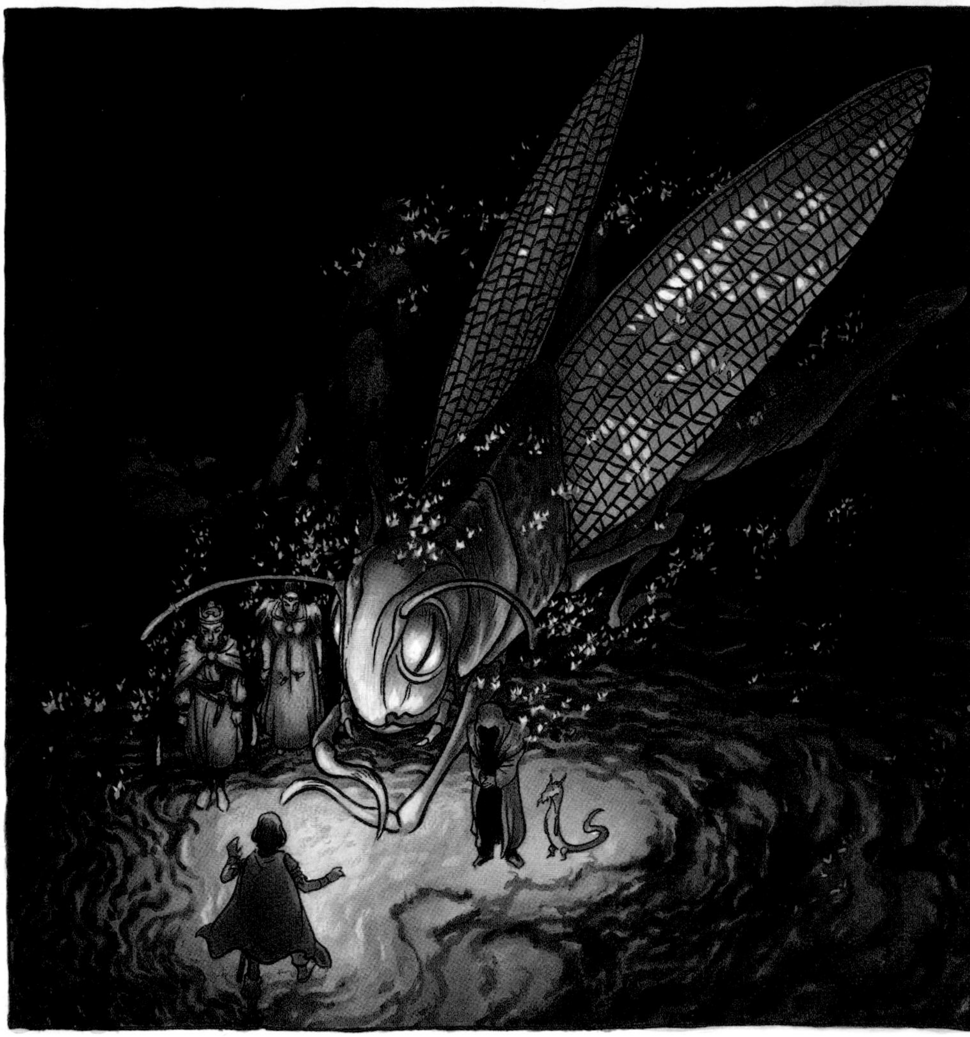

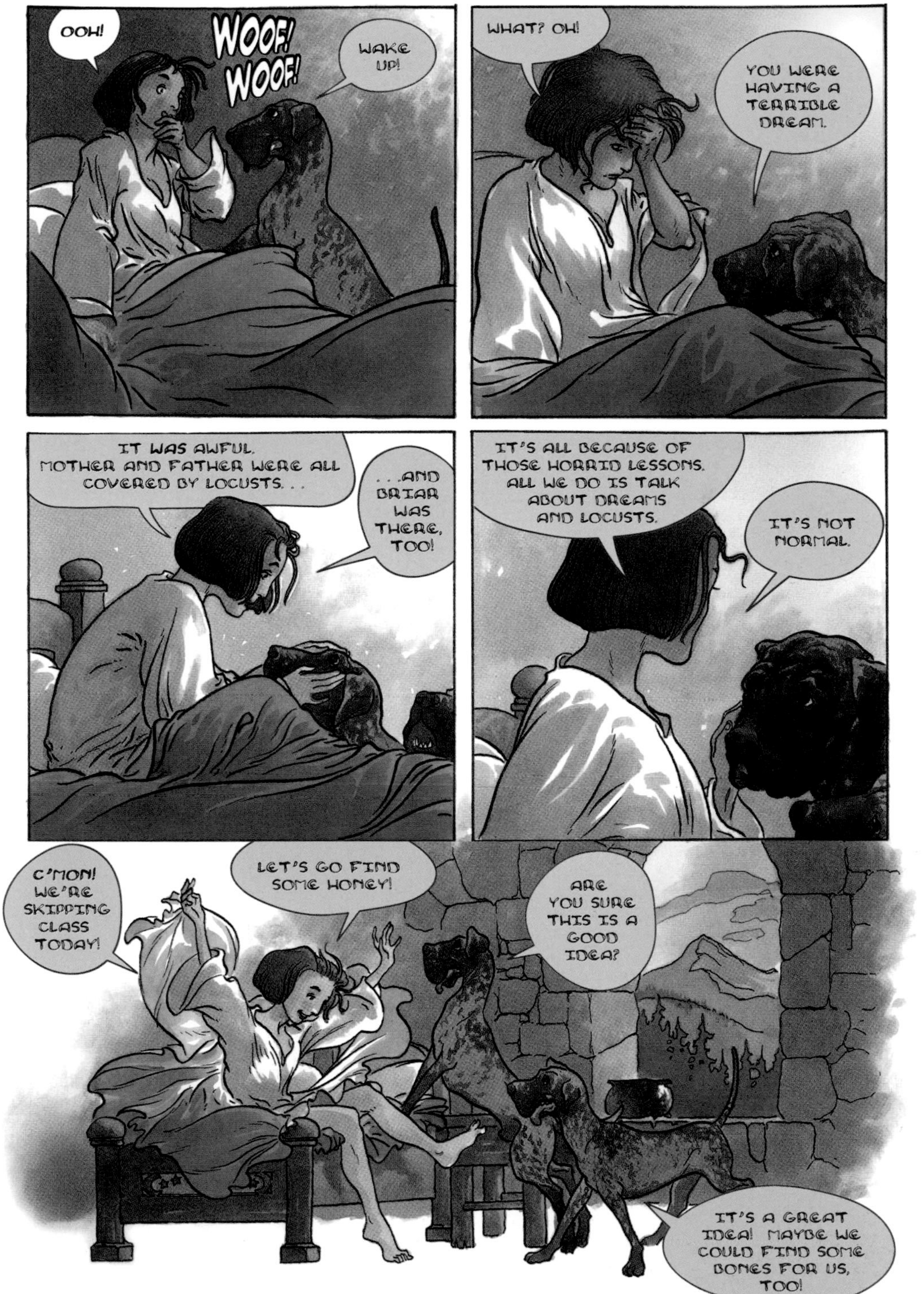
OOH!
WOOF! WOOF!
WAKE UP!
WHAT? OH!
YOU WERE HAVING A TERRIBLE DREAM.
IT WAS AWFUL. MOTHER AND FATHER WERE ALL COVERED BY LOCUSTS. . .
. . .AND BRIAR WAS THERE, TOO!
IT'S ALL BECAUSE OF THOSE HORRID LESSONS. ALL WE DO IS TALK ABOUT DREAMS AND LOCUSTS.
IT'S NOT NORMAL.
C'MON! WE'RE SKIPPING CLASS TODAY!
LET'S GO FIND SOME HONEY!
ARE YOU SURE THIS IS A GOOD IDEA?
IT'S A GREAT IDEA! MAYBE WE COULD FIND SOME BONES FOR US, TOO!

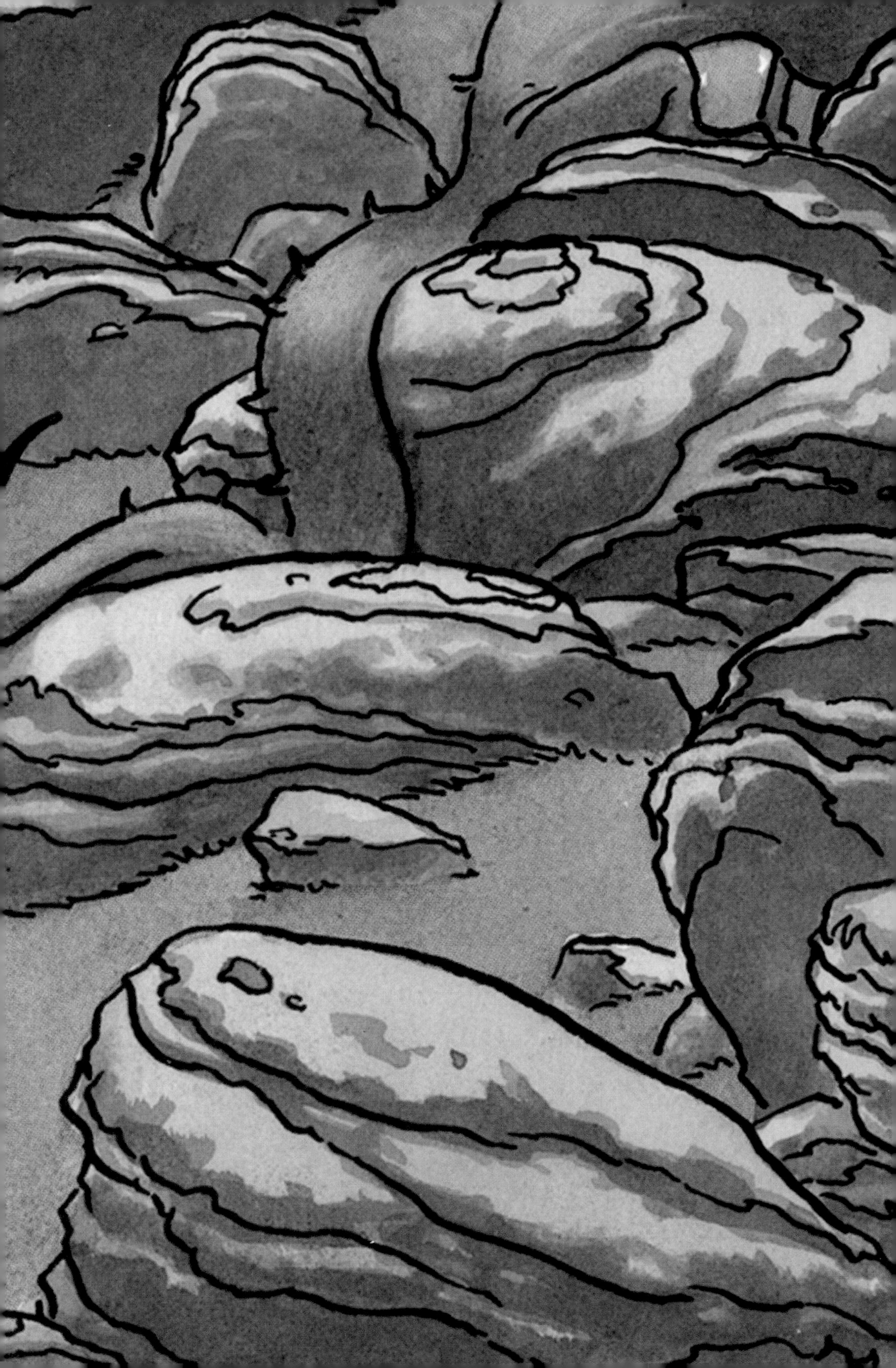

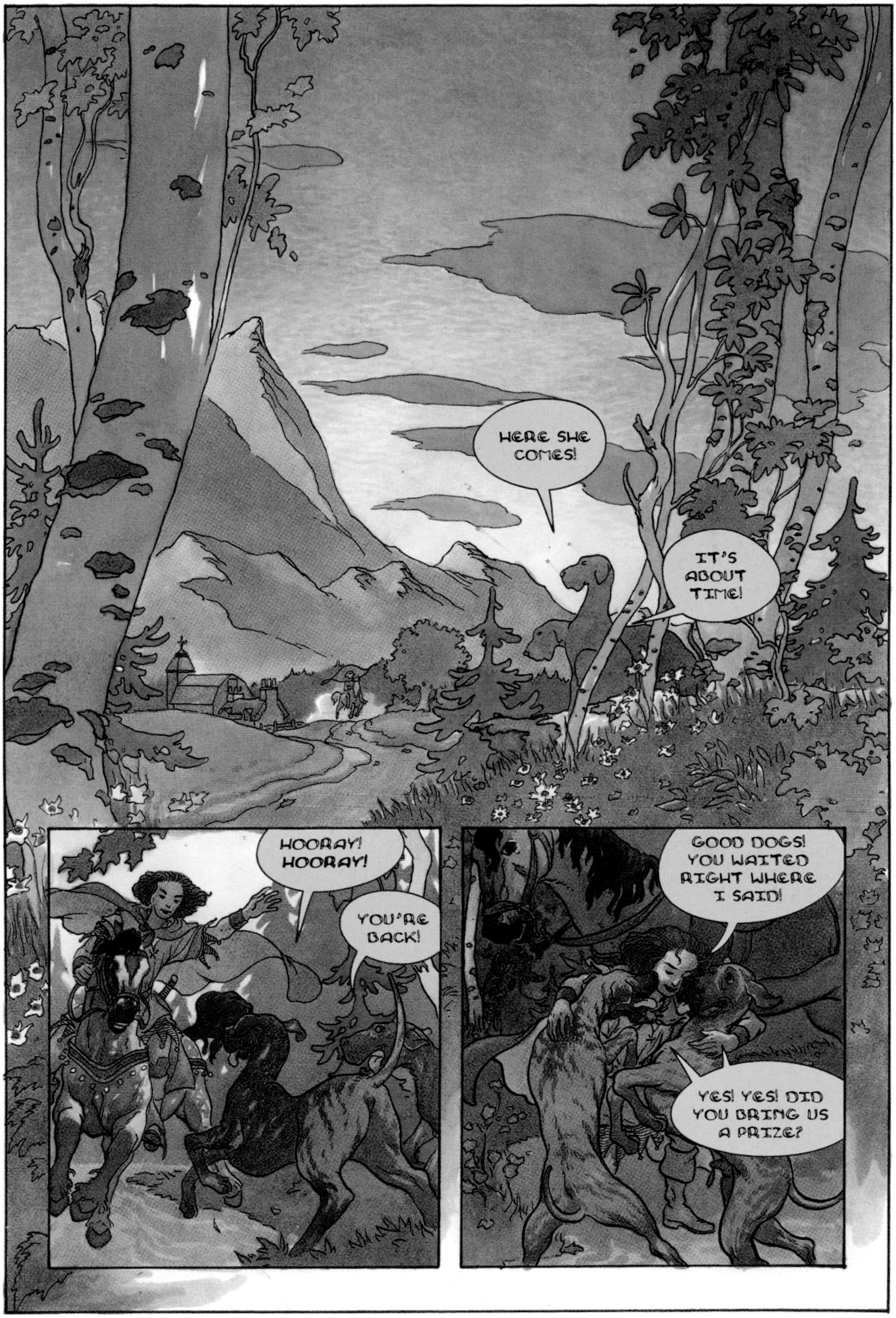
HERE SHE COMES!
IT'S ABOUT TIME!
HOORAY! HOORAY!
YOU'RE BACK!
GOOD DOGS! YOU WAITED RIGHT WHERE I SAID!
YES! YES! DID YOU BRING US A PRIZE?

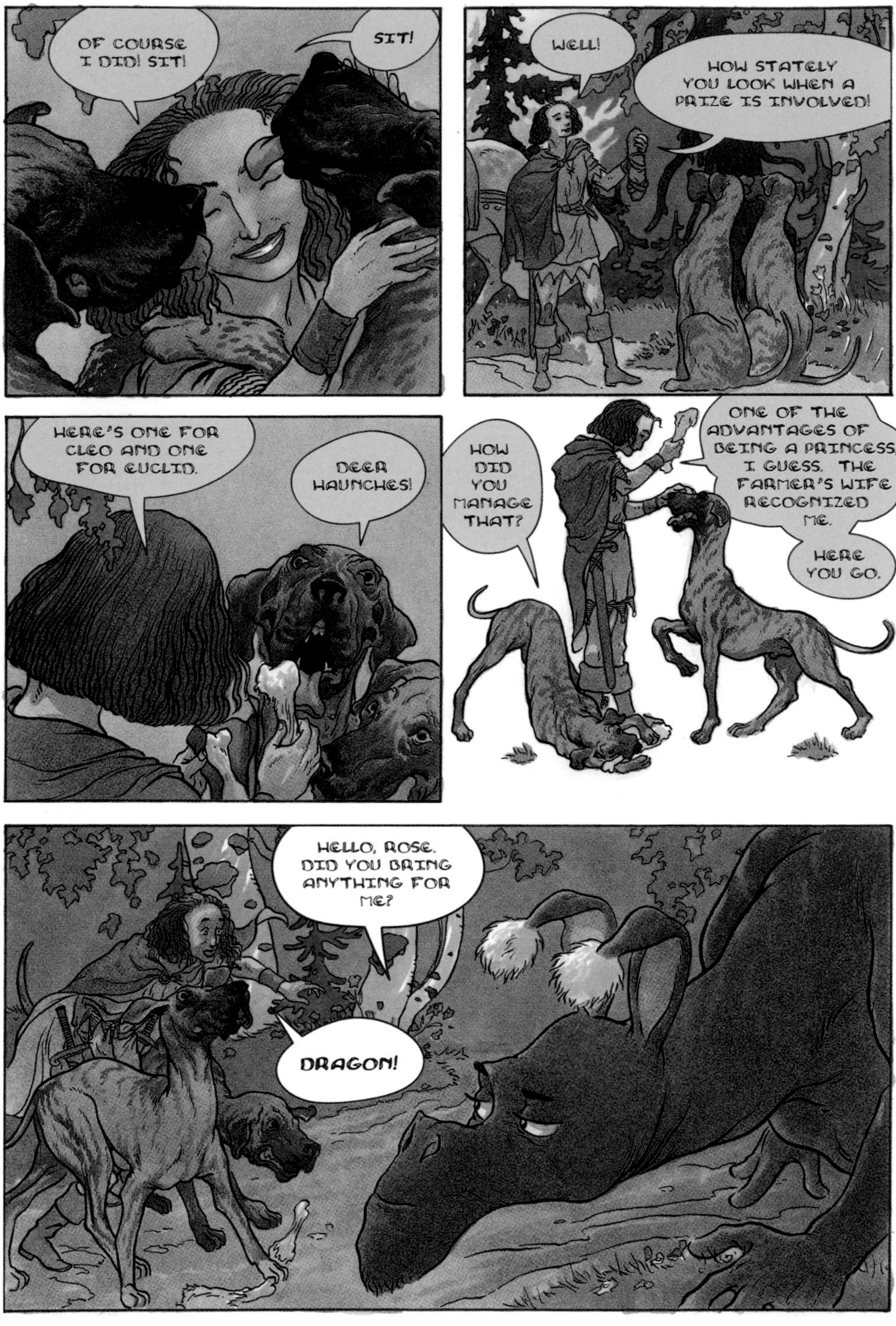
OF COURSE I DID! SIT!
SIT!
WELL!
HOW STATELY YOU LOOK WHEN A PRIZE IS INVOLVED!
HERE'S ONE FOR CLEO AND ONE FOR EUCLID.
DEER HAUNCHES!
HOW DID YOU MANAGE THAT?
ONE OF THE ADVANTAGES OF BEING A PRINCESS, I GUESS. THE FARMER'S WIFE RECOGNIZED ME.
HERE YOU GO.
HELLO, ROSE. DID YOU BRING ANYTHING FOR ME?
DRAGON!

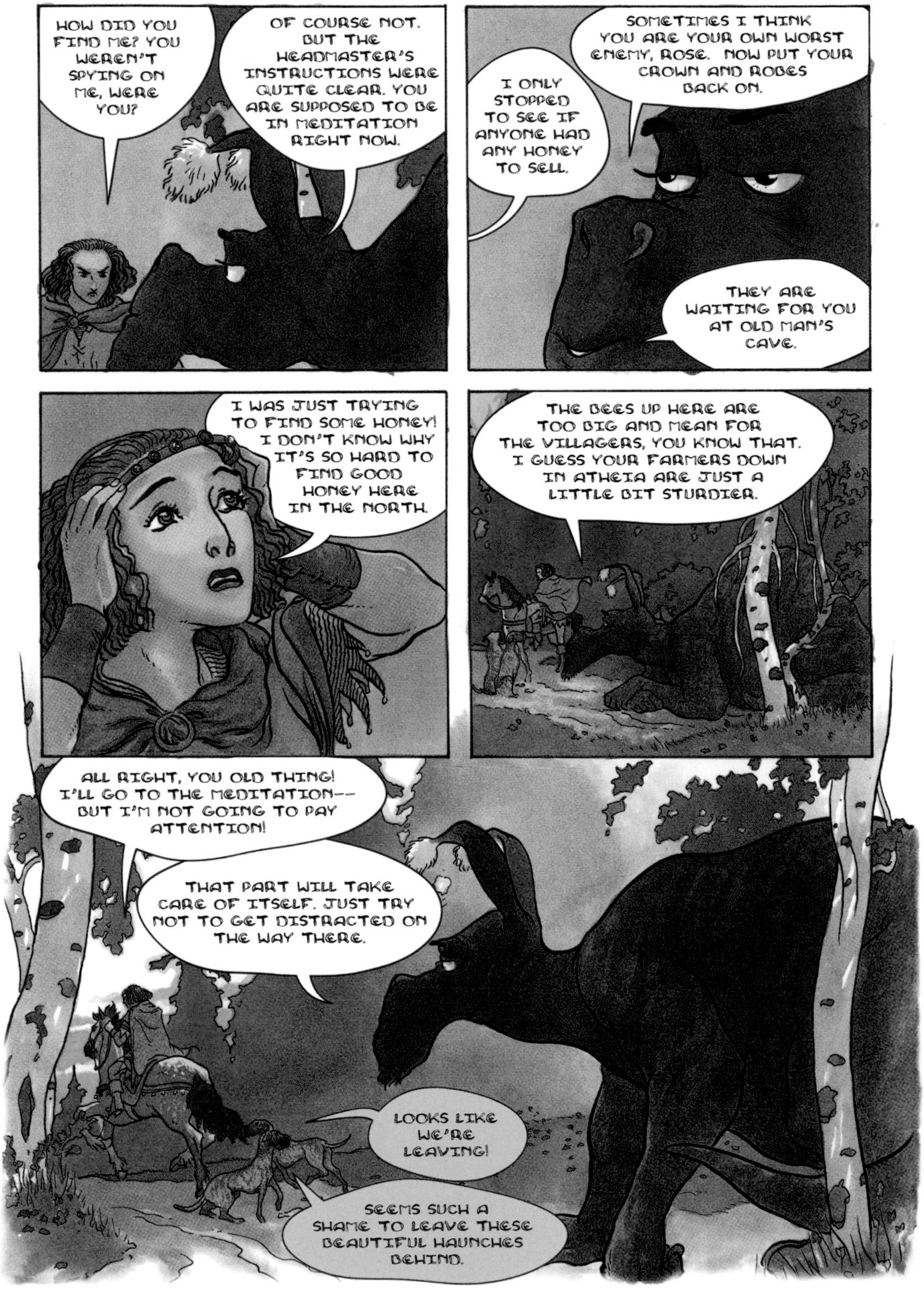
HOW DID YOU FIND ME? YOU WEREN'T SPYING ON ME, WERE YOU?
OF COURSE NOT. BUT THE HEADMASTER'S INSTRUCTIONS WERE QUITE CLEAR. YOU ARE SUPPOSED TO BE IN MEDITATION RIGHT NOW.
I ONLY STOPPED TO SEE IF ANYONE HAD ANY HONEY TO SELL.
SOMETIMES I THINK YOU ARE YOUR OWN WORST ENEMY, ROSE. NOW PUT YOUR CROWN AND ROBES BACK ON.
THEY ARE WAITING FOR YOU AT OLD MAN'S CAVE.
I WAS JUST TRYING TO FIND SOME HONEY! I DON'T KNOW WHY IT'S SO HARD TO FIND GOOD HONEY HERE IN THE NORTH.
THE BEES UP HERE ARE TOO BIG AND MEAN FOR THE VILLAGERS, YOU KNOW THAT. I GUESS YOUR FARMERS DOWN IN ATHEIA ARE JUST A LITTLE BIT STURDIER.
ALL RIGHT, YOU OLD THING! I'LL GO TO THE MEDITATION-- BUT I'M NOT GOING TO PAY ATTENTION!
THAT PART WILL TAKE CARE OF ITSELF. JUST TRY NOT TO GET DISTRACTED ON THE WAY THERE.
LOOKS LIKE WE'RE LEAVING!
SEEMS SUCH A SHAME TO LEAVE THESE BEAUTIFUL HAUNCHES BEHIND.

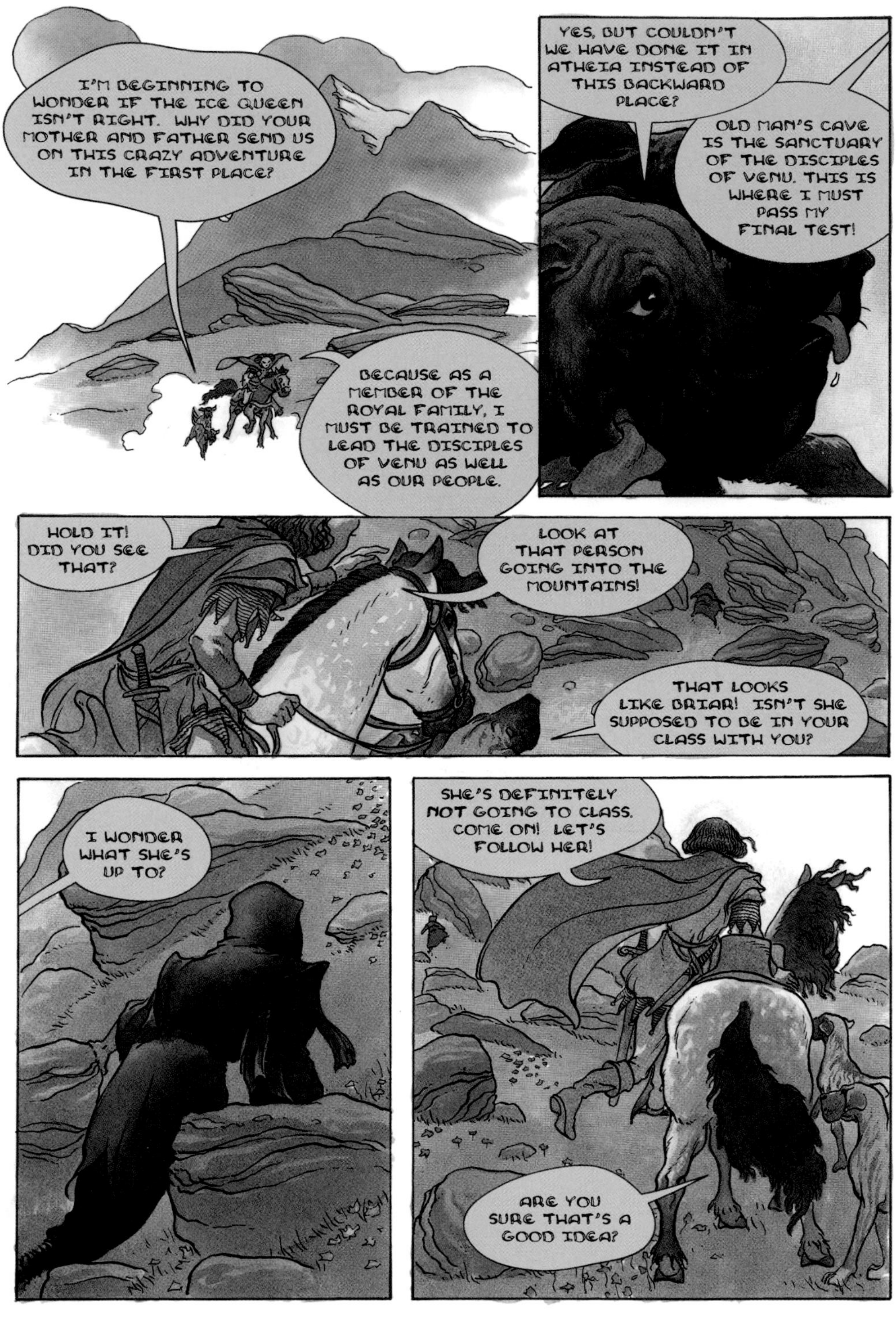
I'M BEGINNING TO WONDER IF THE ICE QUEEN ISN'T RIGHT. WHY DID YOUR MOTHER AND FATHER SEND US ON THIS CRAZY ADVENTURE IN THE FIRST PLACE?
BECAUSE AS A MEMBER OF THE ROYAL FAMILY, I MUST BE TRAINED TO LEAD THE DISCIPLES OF VENU AS WELL AS OUR PEOPLE.
YES, BUT COULDN'T WE HAVE DONE IT IN ATHEIA INSTEAD OF THIS BACKWARD PLACE?
OLD MAN'S CAVE IS THE SANCTUARY OF THE DISCIPLES OF VENU. THIS IS WHERE I MUST PASS MY FINAL TEST!
HOLD IT! DID YOU SEE THAT?
LOOK AT THAT PERSON GOING INTO THE MOUNTAINS!
THAT LOOKS LIKE BRIAR! ISN'T SHE SUPPOSED TO BE IN YOUR CLASS WITH YOU?
I WONDER WHAT SHE'S UP TO?
SHE'S DEFINITELY NOT GOING TO CLASS. COME ON! LET'S FOLLOW HER!
ARE YOU SURE THAT'S A GOOD IDEA?

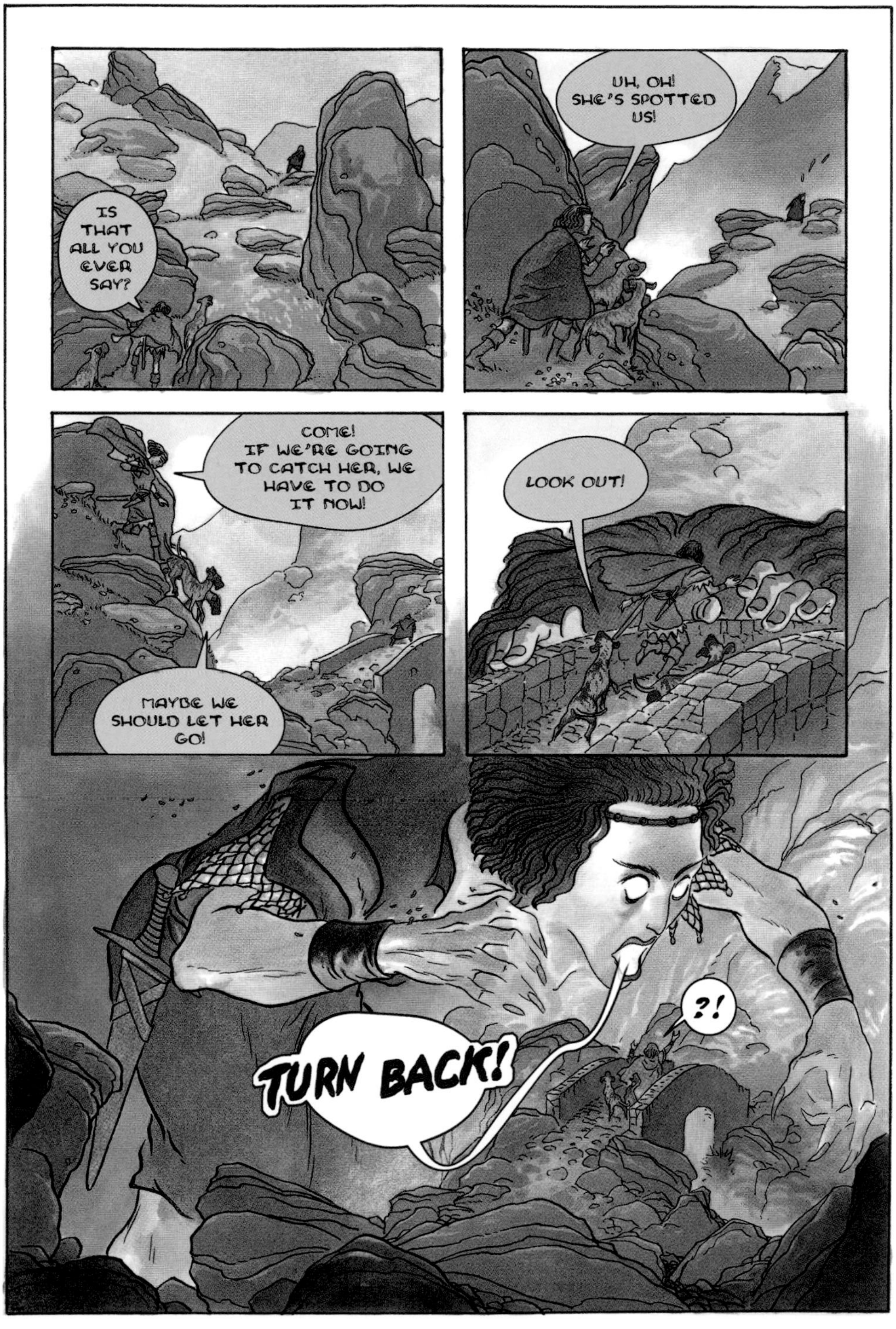
IS THAT ALL YOU EVER SAY?
UH, OH! SHE'S SPOTTED US!
COME! IF WE'RE GOING TO CATCH HER, WE HAVE TO DO IT NOW!
MAYBE WE SHOULD LET HER GO!
LOOK OUT!
TURN BACK!
?!

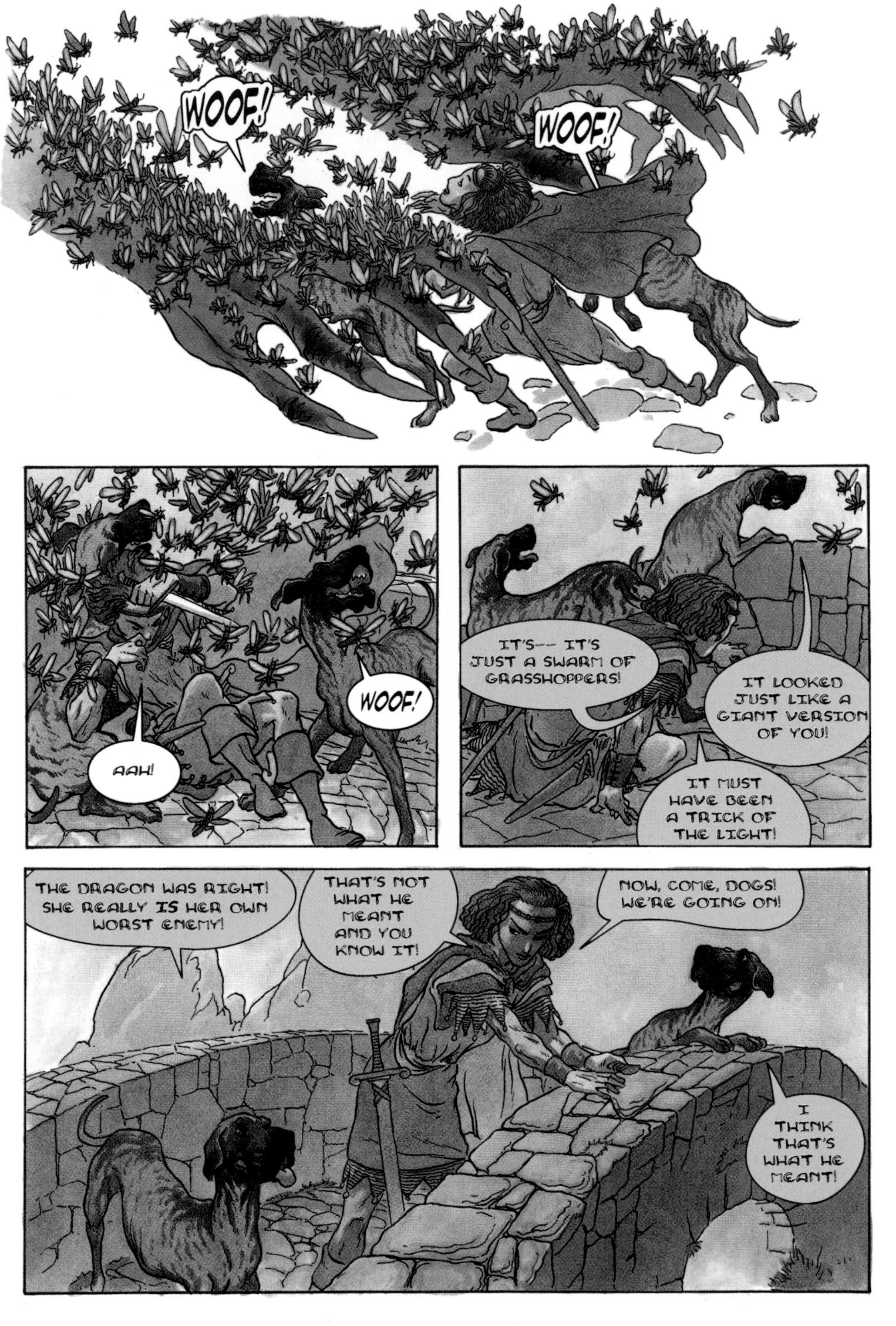
WOOF!
WOOF!
AAH!
WOOF!
IT'S-- IT'S JUST A SWARM OF GRASSHOPPERS!
IT LOOKED JUST LIKE A GIANT VERSION OF YOU!
IT MUST HAVE BEEN A TRICK OF THE LIGHT!
THE DRAGON WAS RIGHT! SHE REALLY IS HER OWN WORST ENEMY!
THAT'S NOT WHAT HE MEANT AND YOU KNOW IT!
NOW, COME, DOGS! WE'RE GOING ON!
I THINK THAT'S WHAT HE MEANT!

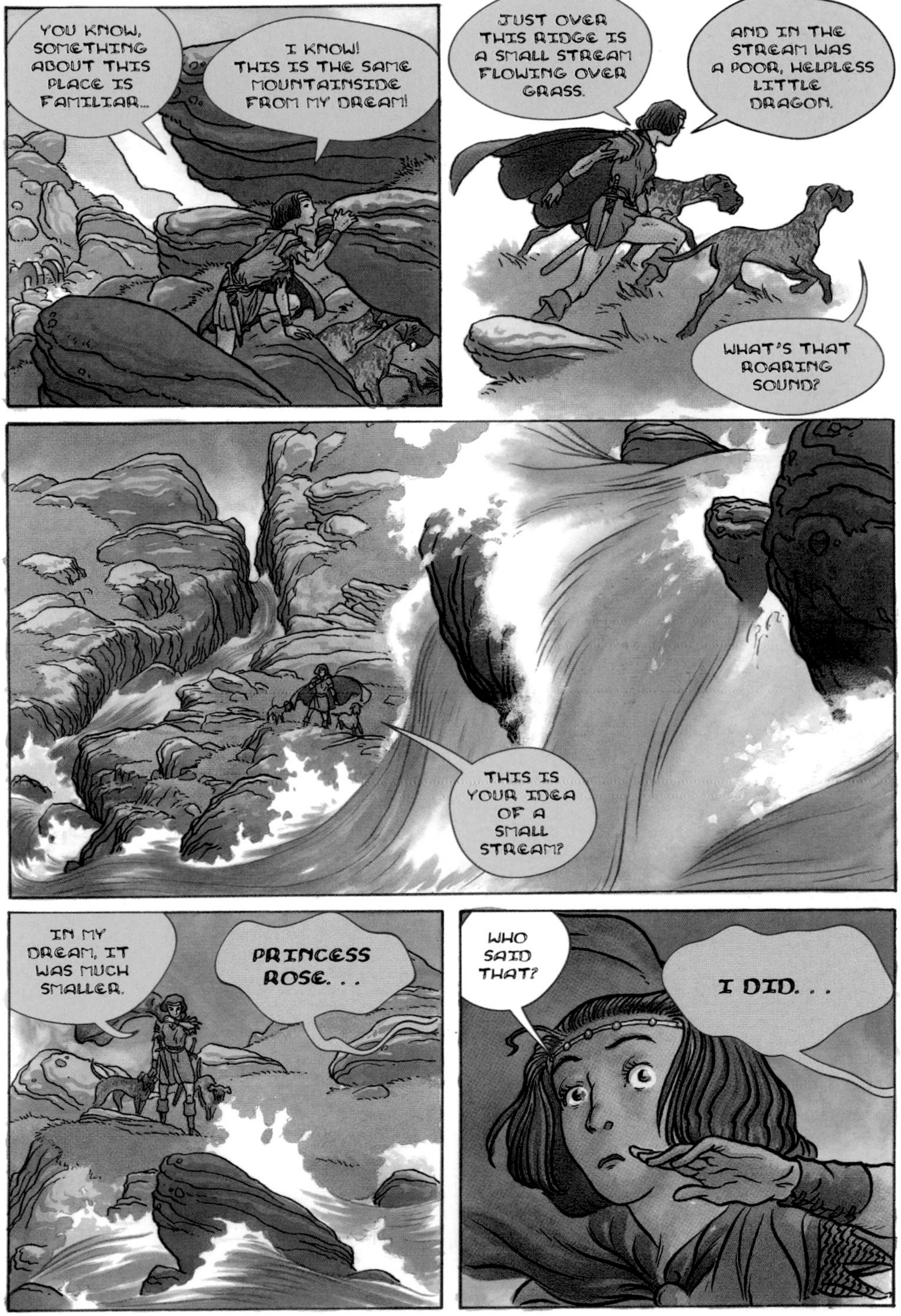
YOU KNOW, SOMETHING ABOUT THIS PLACE IS FAMILIAR...
I KNOW! THIS IS THE SAME MOUNTAINSIDE FROM MY DREAM!
JUST OVER THIS RIDGE IS A SMALL STREAM FLOWING OVER GRASS.
AND IN THE STREAM WAS A POOR, HELPLESS LITTLE DRAGON.
WHAT'S THAT ROARING SOUND?
THIS IS YOUR IDEA OF A SMALL STREAM?
IN MY DREAM, IT WAS MUCH SMALLER.
PRINCESS ROSE. . .
WHO SAID THAT?
I DID. . .

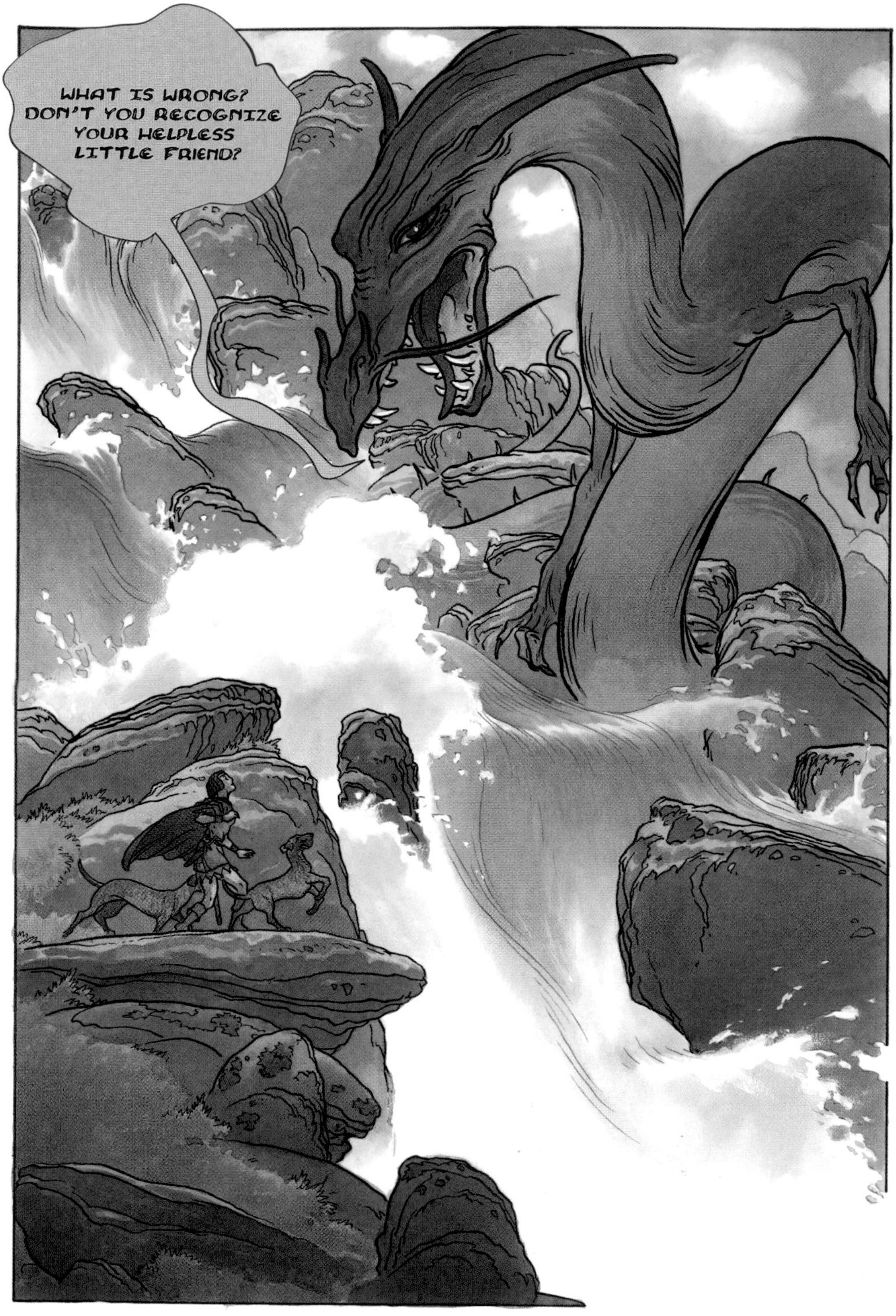
WHAT IS WRONG?
DON'T YOU RECOGNIZE
YOUR HELPLESS
LITTLE FRIEND?

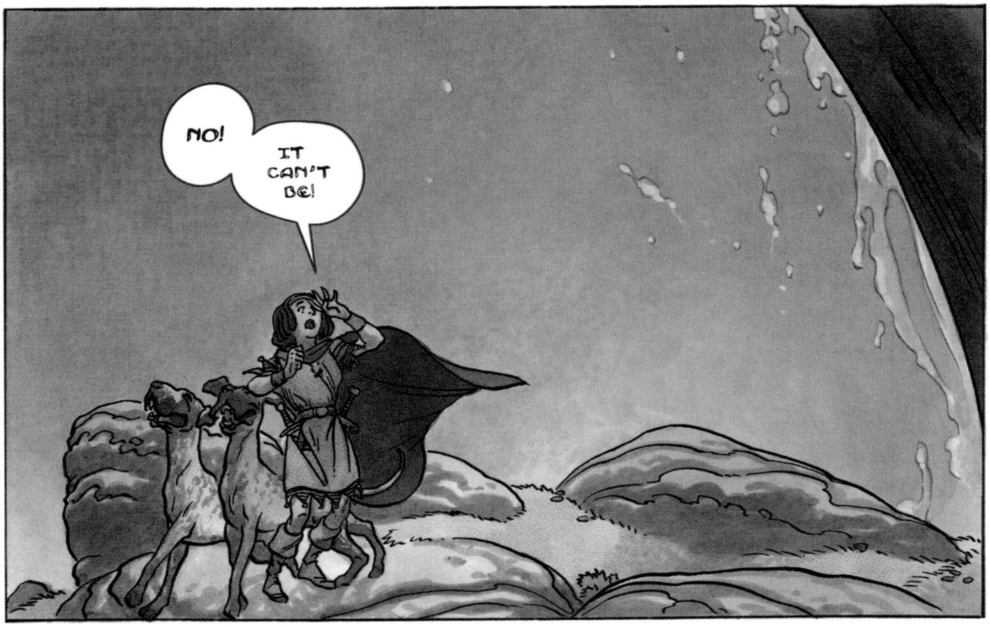
NO!
IT CAN'T BE!

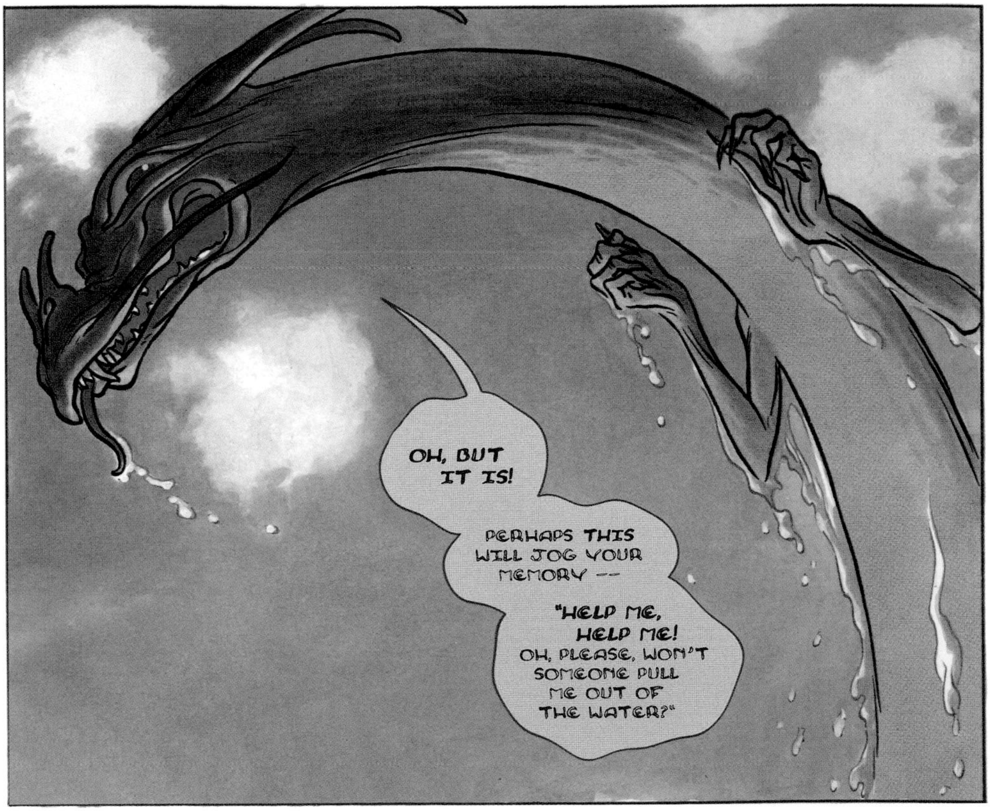
OH, BUT IT IS!
PERHAPS THIS WILL JOG YOUR MEMORY --
"HELP ME, HELP ME! OH, PLEASE, WON'T SOMEONE PULL ME OUT OF THE WATER?"

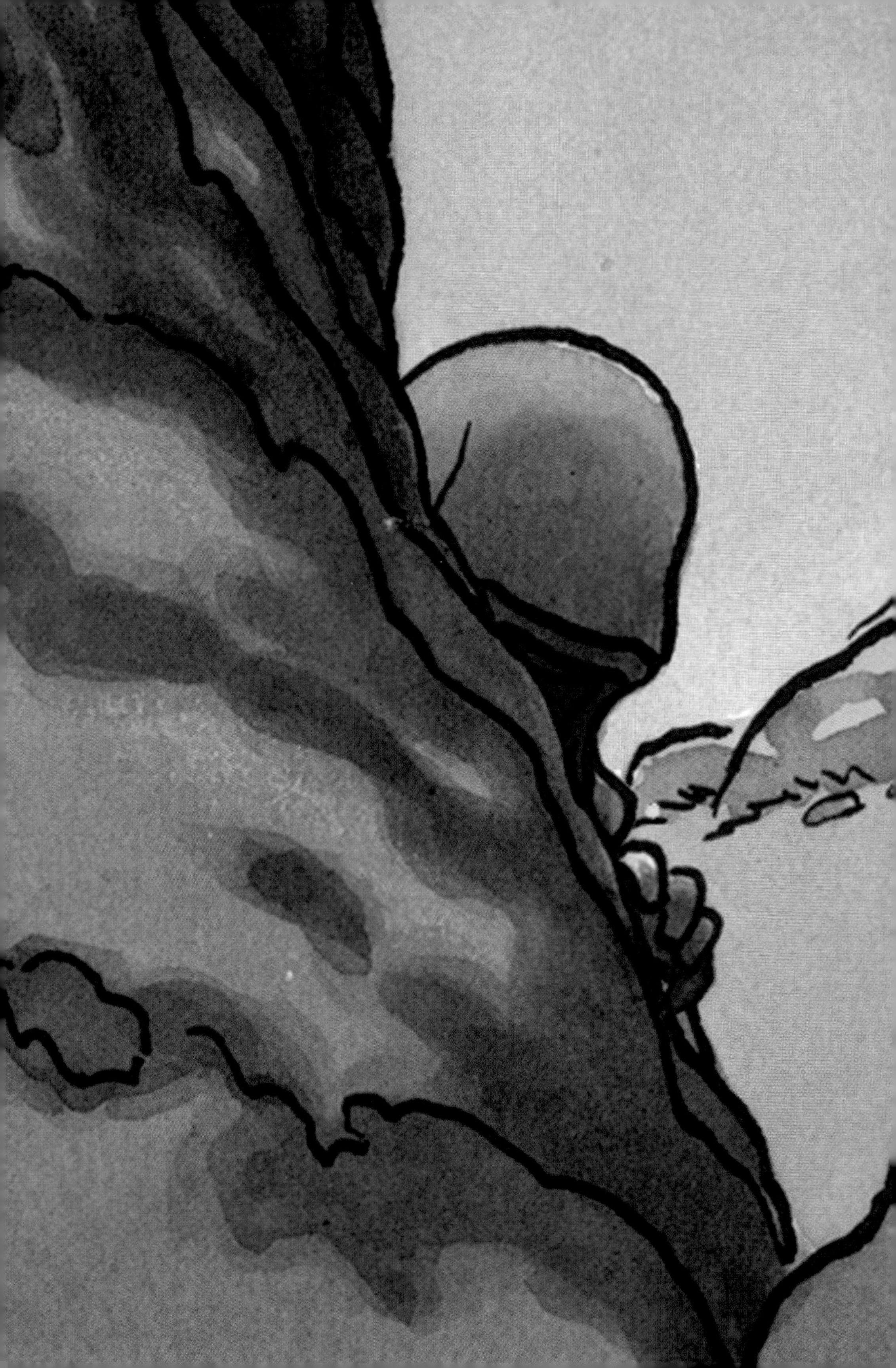

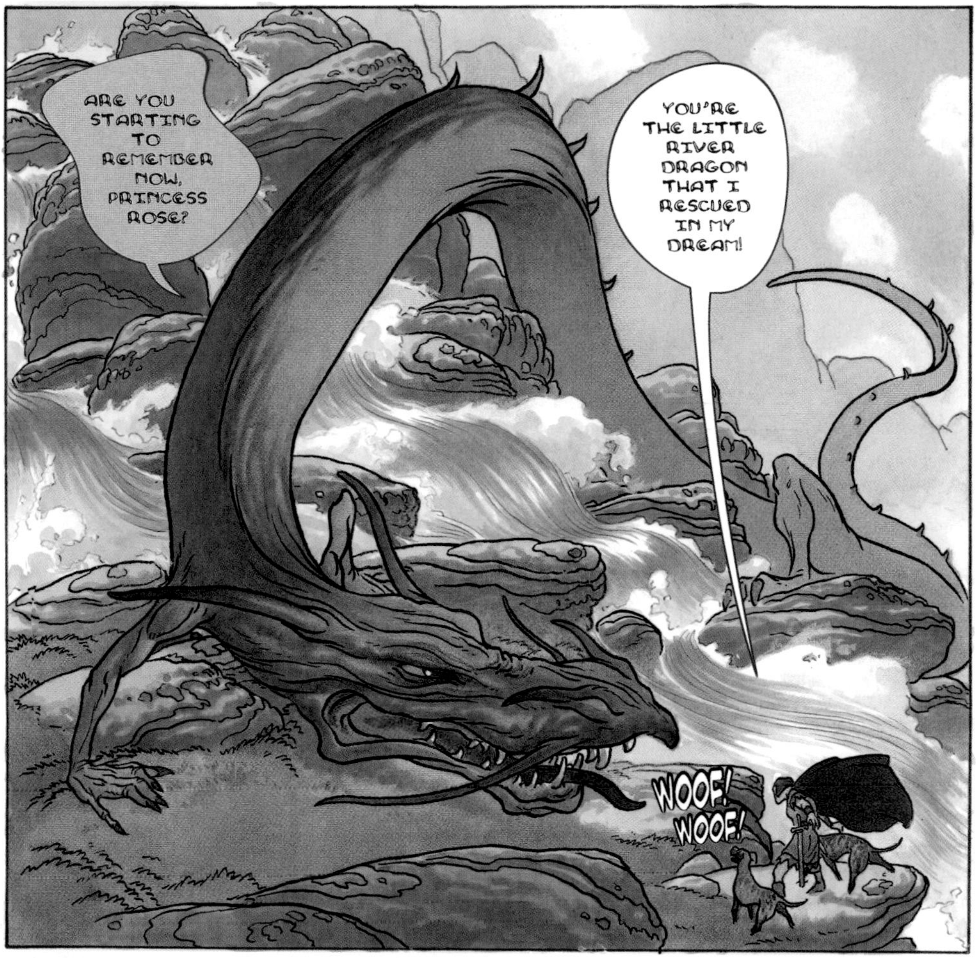
ARE YOU STARTING TO REMEMBER NOW, PRINCESS ROSE?
YOU'RE THE LITTLE RIVER DRAGON THAT I RESCUED IN MY DREAM!
WOOF! WOOF!

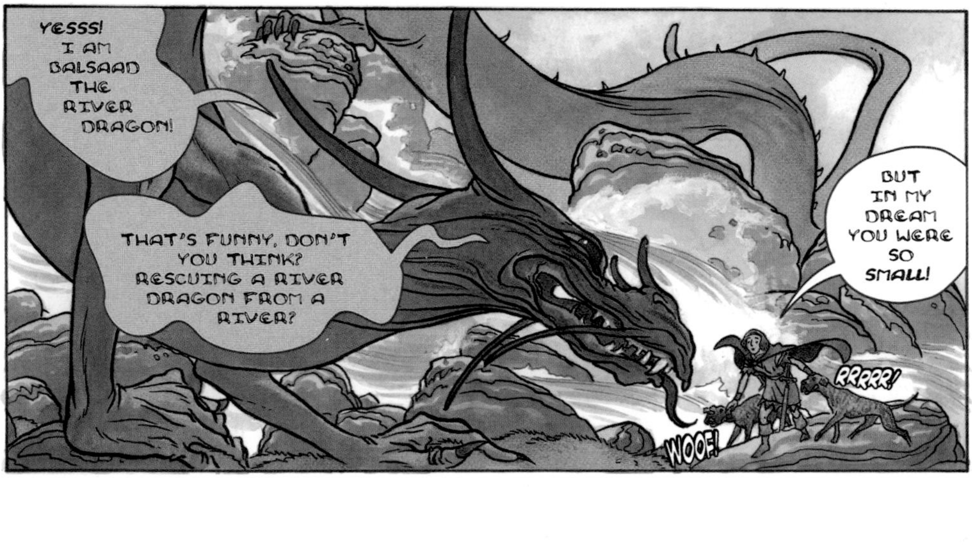
YESSS! I AM BALSAAD THE RIVER DRAGON!
THAT'S FUNNY, DON'T YOU THINK? RESCUING A RIVER DRAGON FROM A RIVER?
BUT IN MY DREAM YOU WERE SO SMALL!
RRRRR!
WOOF!

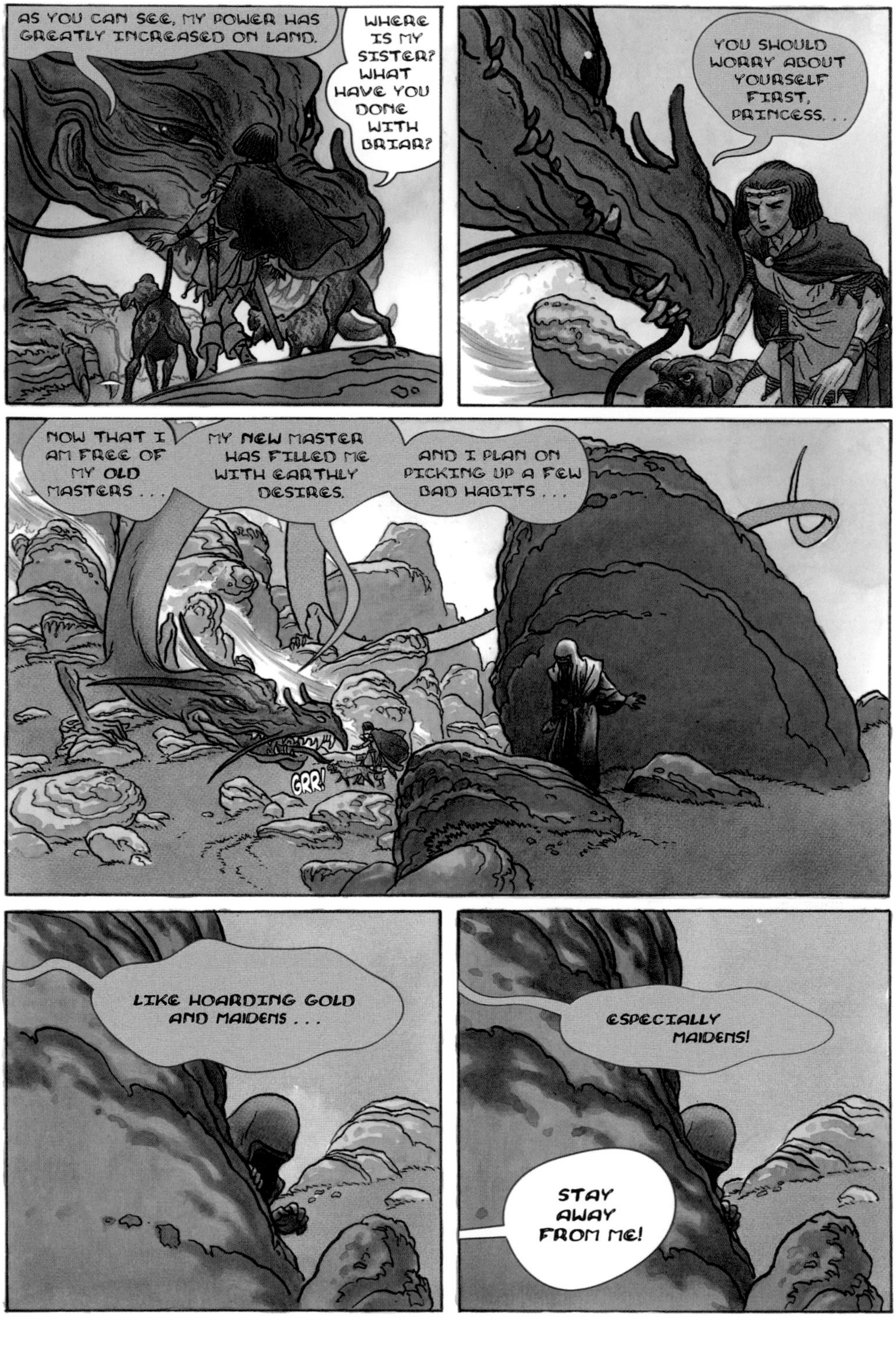
AS YOU CAN SEE, MY POWER HAS GREATLY INCREASED ON LAND.
WHERE IS MY SISTER? WHAT HAVE YOU DONE WITH BRIAR?
YOU SHOULD WORRY ABOUT YOURSELF FIRST, PRINCESS. . .
NOW THAT I AM FREE OF MY OLD MASTERS . . .
MY NEW MASTER HAS FILLED ME WITH EARTHLY DESIRES.
AND I PLAN ON PICKING UP A FEW BAD HABITS . . .
GRR!
LIKE HOARDING GOLD AND MAIDENS . . .
ESPECIALLY MAIDENS!
STAY AWAY FROM ME!

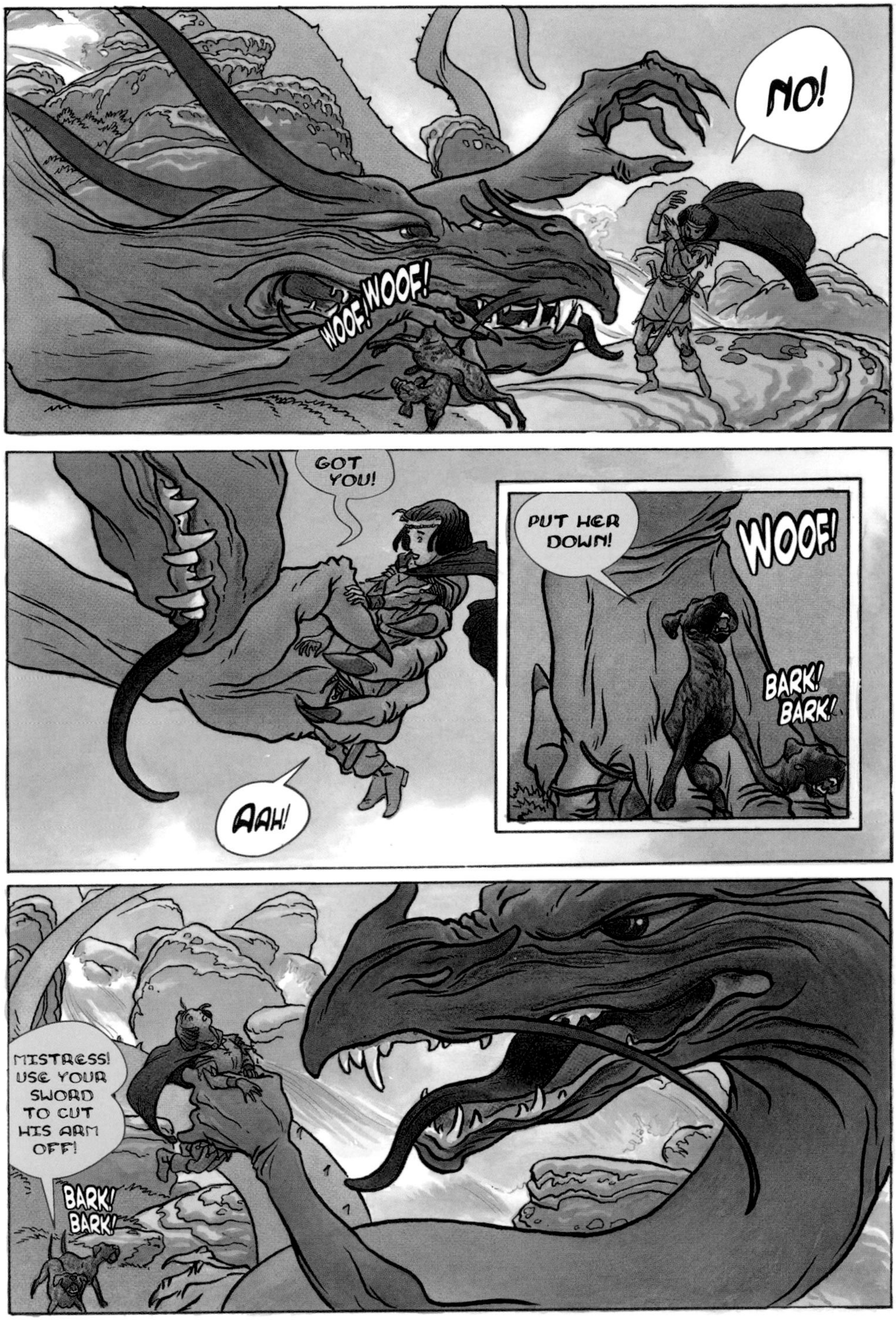
NO!
WOOF! WOOF!
GOT YOU!
AAH!
PUT HER DOWN!
WOOF!
BARK! BARK!
MISTRESS! USE YOUR SWORD TO CUT HIS ARM OFF!
BARK! BARK!

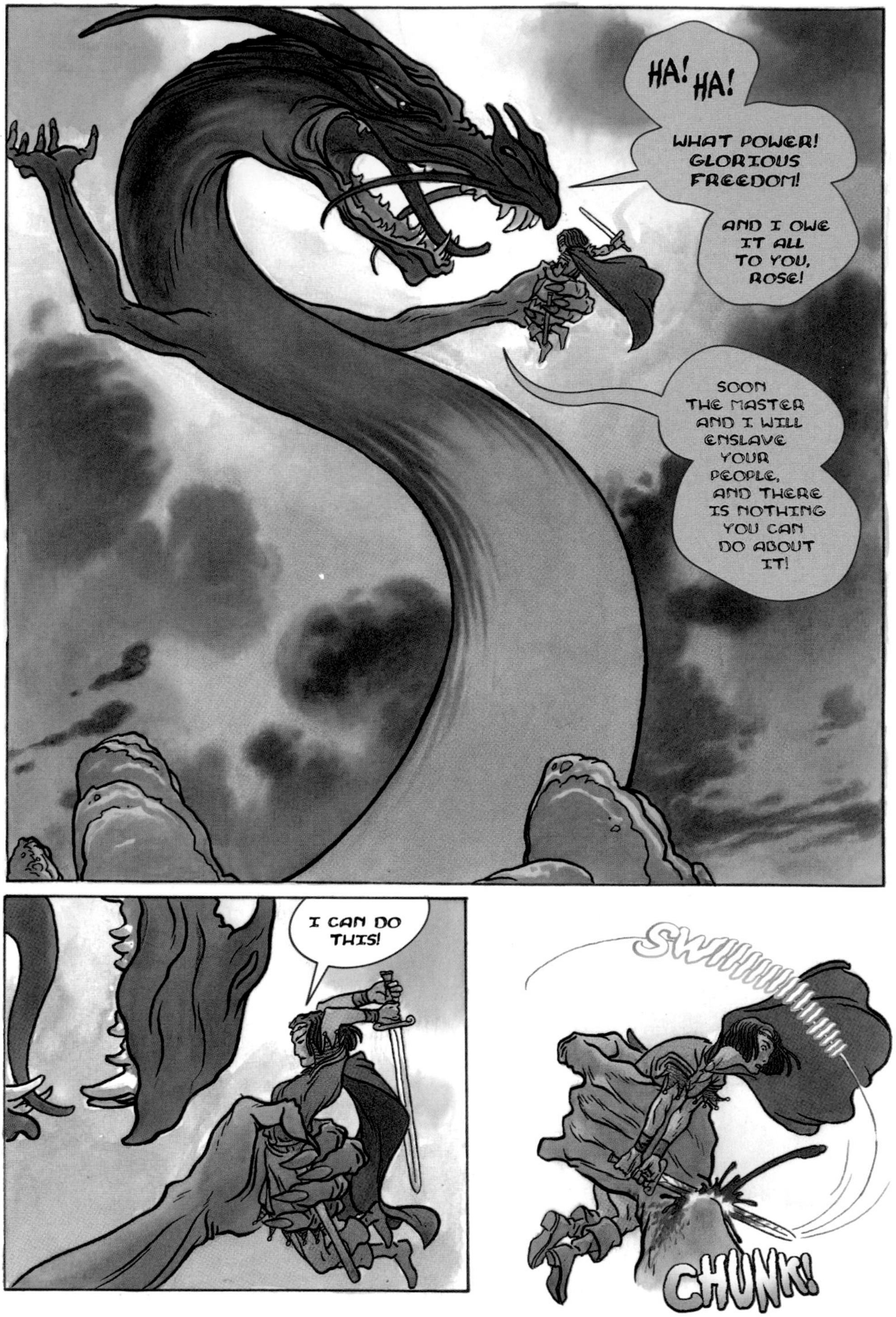
HA! HA!
WHAT POWER! GLORIOUS FREEDOM!
AND I OWE IT ALL TO YOU, ROSE!
SOON THE MASTER AND I WILL ENSLAVE YOUR PEOPLE, AND THERE IS NOTHING YOU CAN DO ABOUT IT!
I CAN DO THIS!
SWIIIIIIIIIIIIIIIIIIIIIIIII
CHUNK!

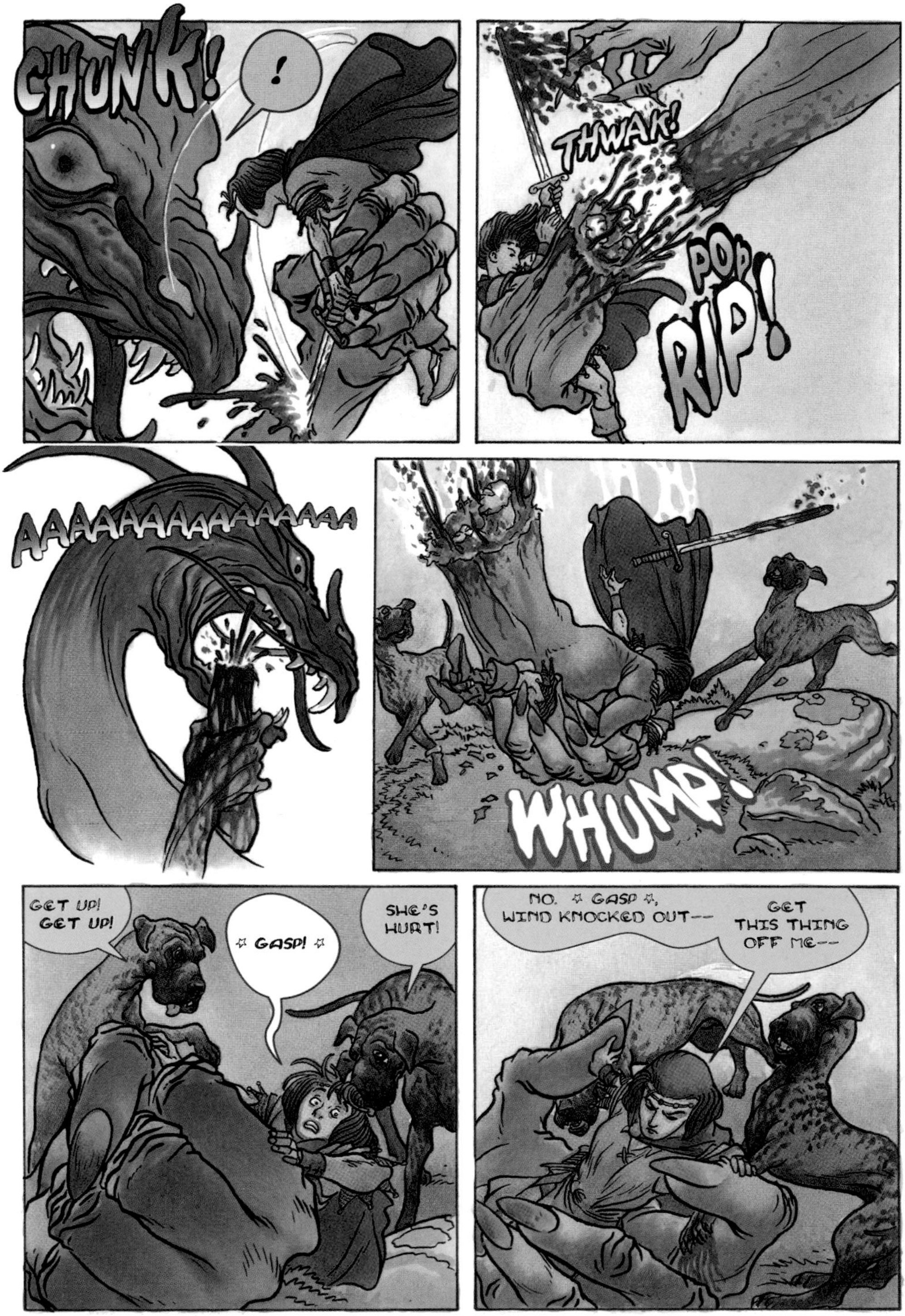
CHUNK!
!
THWAK!
POP
RIP!
AAAAAAAAAAAAAAA
WHUMP!
GET UP! GET UP!
☆ GASP! ☆
SHE'S HURT!
NO. ☆ GASP ☆, WIND KNOCKED OUT--
GET THIS THING OFF ME--

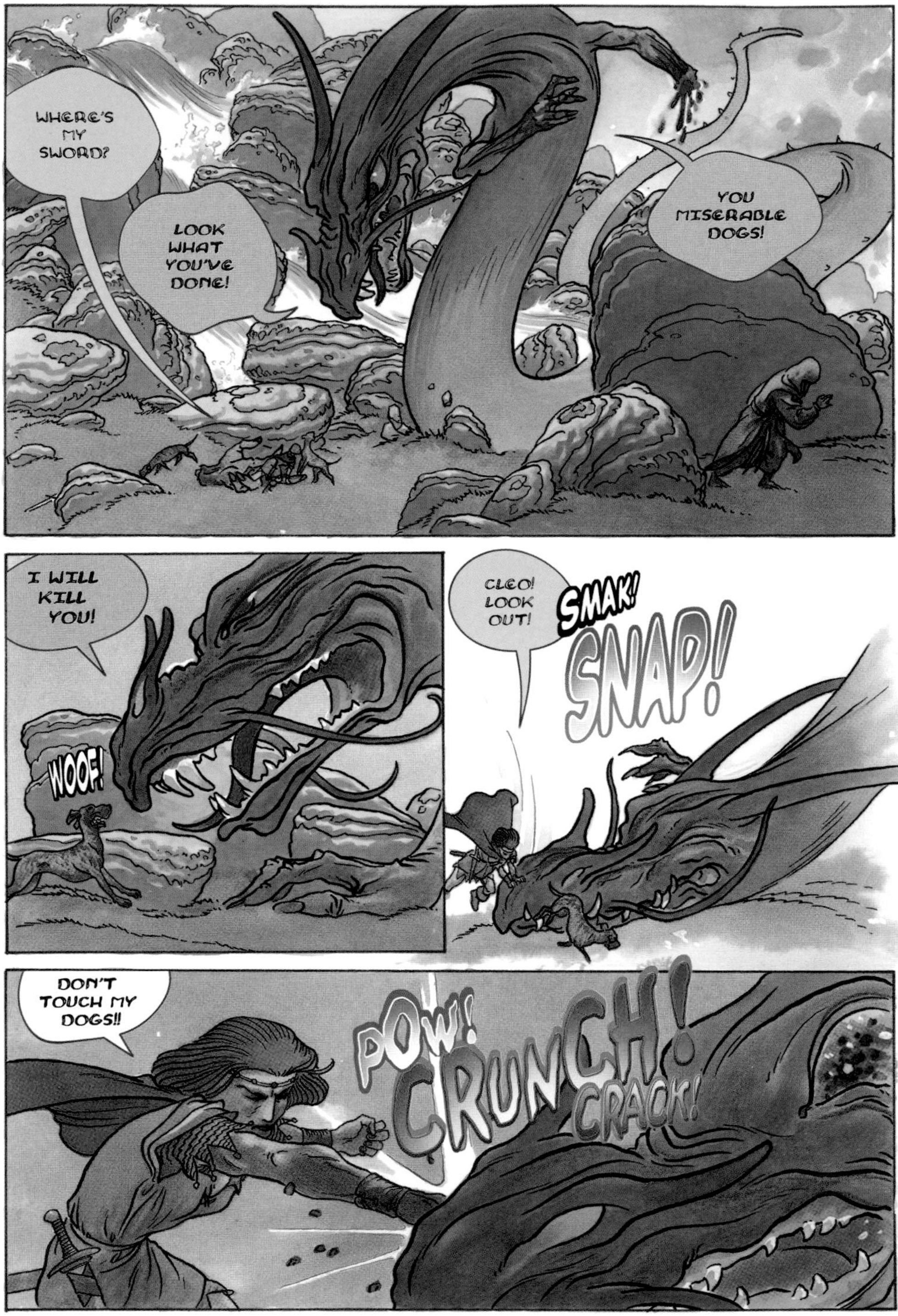
WHERE'S MY SWORD?
LOOK WHAT YOU'VE DONE!
YOU MISERABLE DOGS!
I WILL KILL YOU!
WOOF!
CLEO! LOOK OUT!
SMAK!
SNAP!
DON'T TOUCH MY DOGS!!
POW!
CRUNCH!
CRACK!

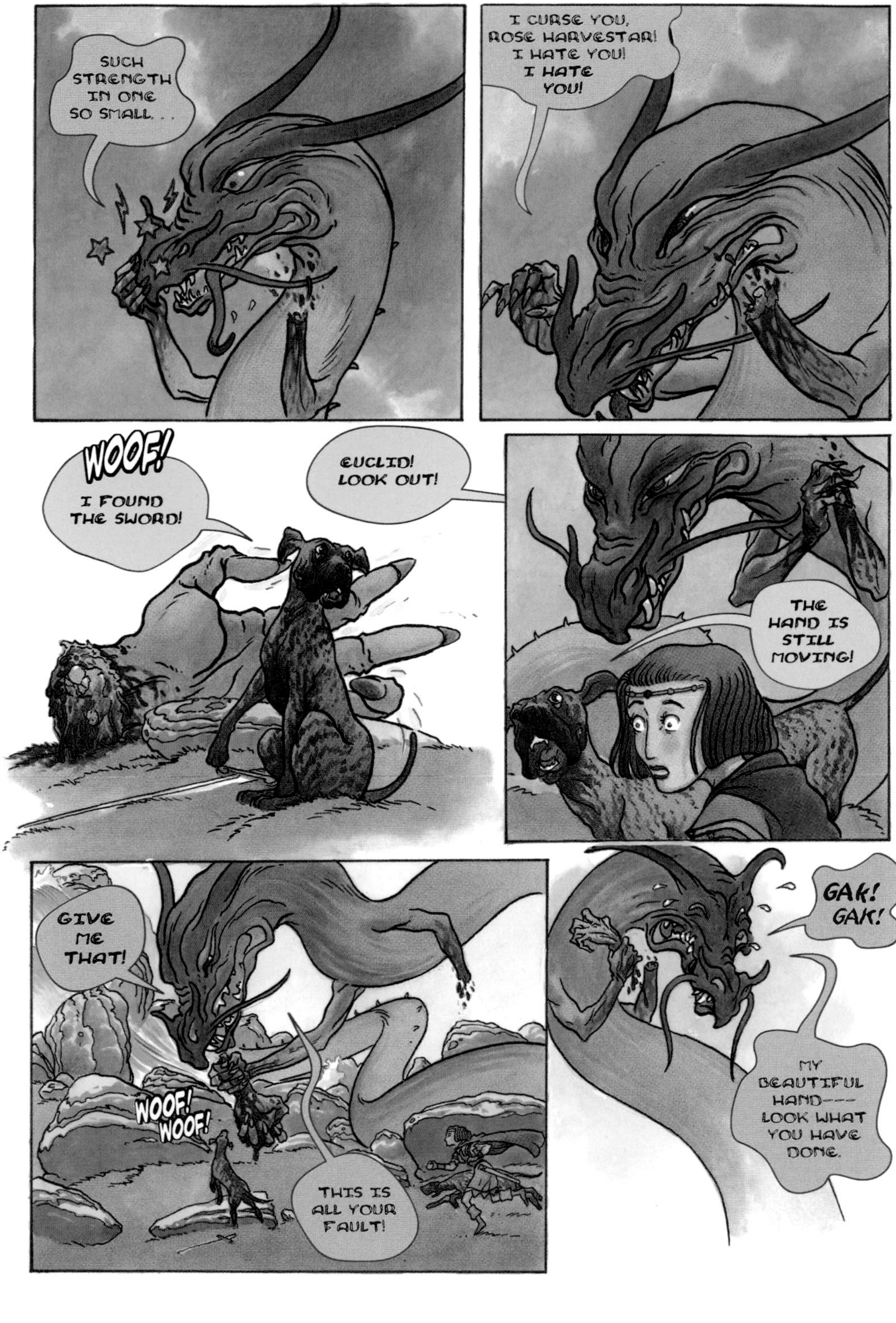
SUCH STRENGTH IN ONE SO SMALL . . .
I CURSE YOU, ROSE HARVESTAR! I HATE YOU! I HATE YOU!
WOOF!
I FOUND THE SWORD!
EUCLID! LOOK OUT!
THE HAND IS STILL MOVING!
GIVE ME THAT!
WOOF! WOOF!
THIS IS ALL YOUR FAULT!
GAK! GAK!
MY BEAUTIFUL HAND--- LOOK WHAT YOU HAVE DONE.

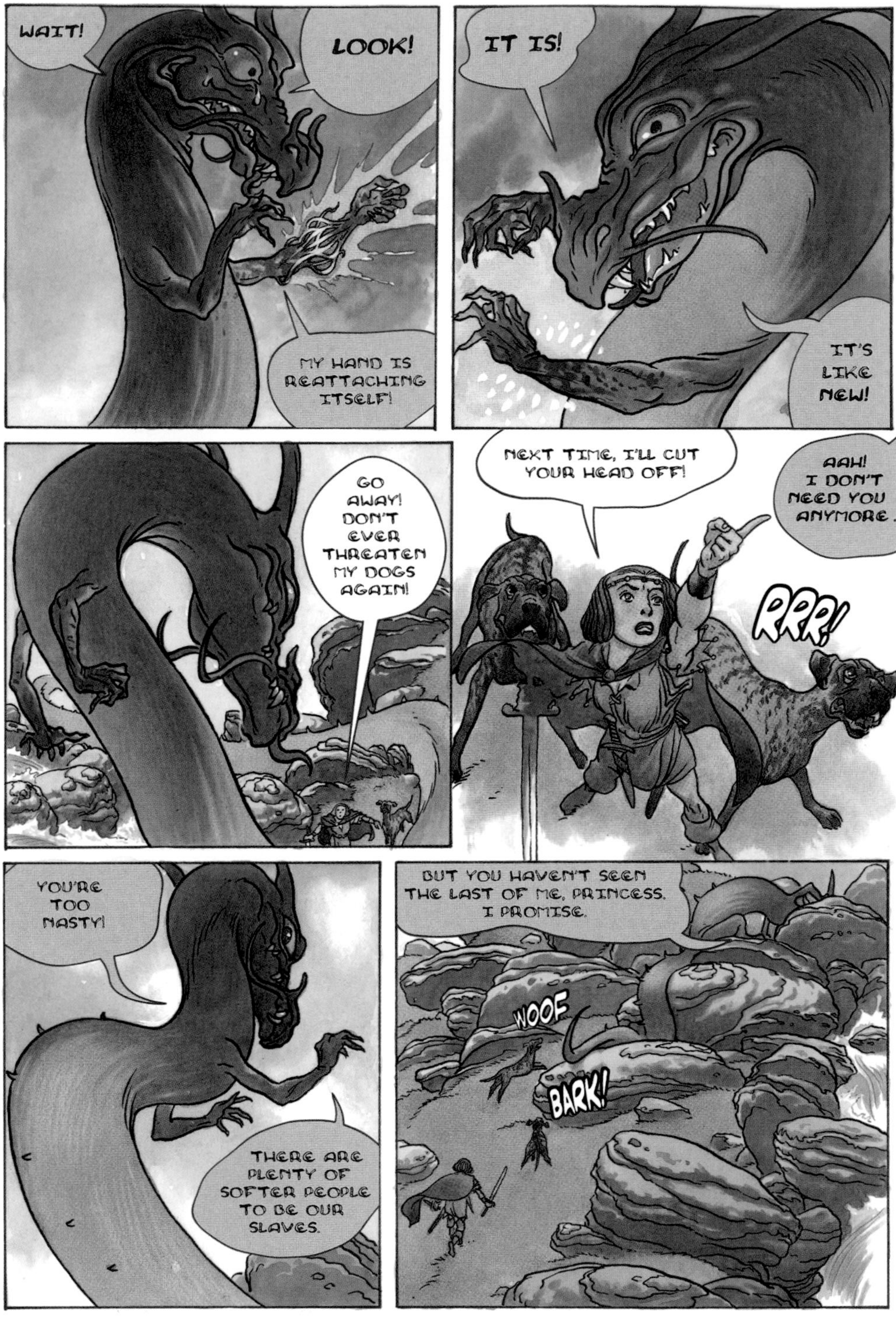
WAIT!
LOOK!
MY HAND IS REATTACHING ITSELF!
IT IS!
IT'S LIKE NEW!
GO AWAY! DON'T EVER THREATEN MY DOGS AGAIN!
NEXT TIME, I'LL CUT YOUR HEAD OFF!
AAH! I DON'T NEED YOU ANYMORE . . .
RRR!
YOU'RE TOO NASTY!
THERE ARE PLENTY OF SOFTER PEOPLE TO BE OUR SLAVES.
BUT YOU HAVEN'T SEEN THE LAST OF ME, PRINCESS. I PROMISE.
WOOF
BARK!

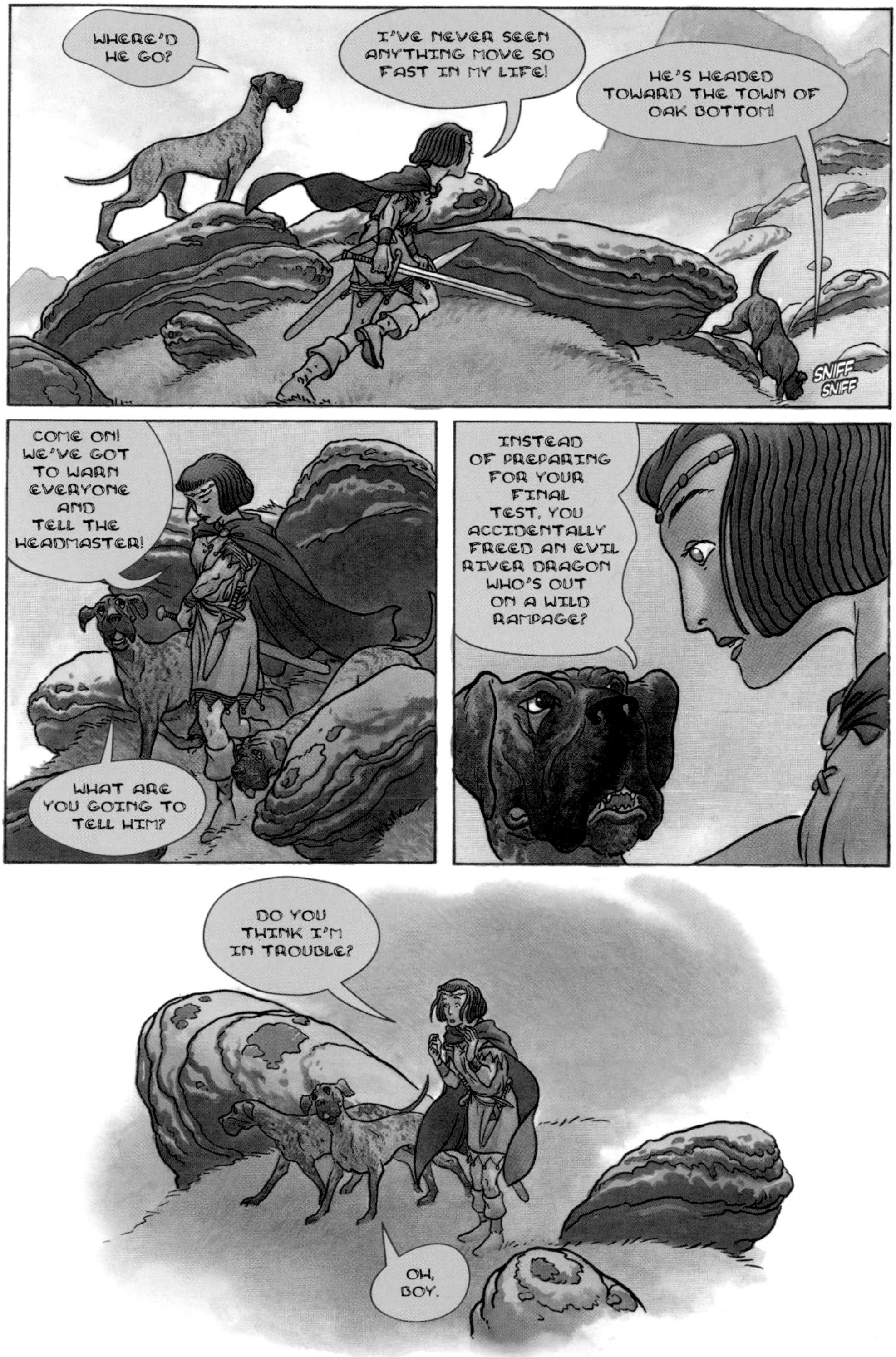
WHERE'D HE GO?
I'VE NEVER SEEN ANYTHING MOVE SO FAST IN MY LIFE!
HE'S HEADED TOWARD THE TOWN OF OAK BOTTOM!
SNIFF SNIFF
COME ON! WE'VE GOT TO WARN EVERYONE AND TELL THE HEADMASTER!
WHAT ARE YOU GOING TO TELL HIM?
INSTEAD OF PREPARING FOR YOUR FINAL TEST, YOU ACCIDENTALLY FREED AN EVIL RIVER DRAGON WHO'S OUT ON A WILD RAMPAGE?
DO YOU THINK I'M IN TROUBLE?
OH, BOY.

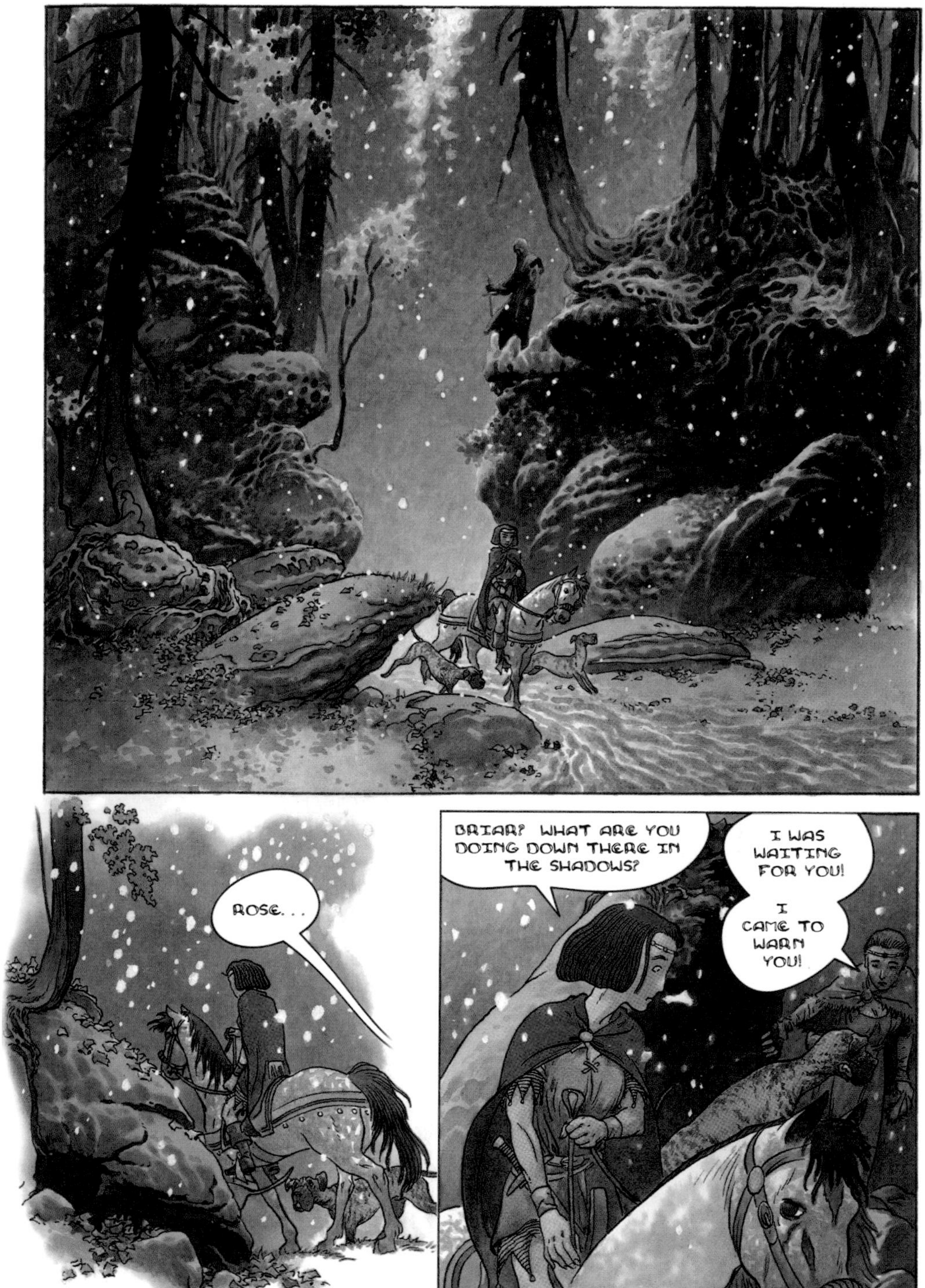
ROSE. . .
BRIAR? WHAT ARE YOU DOING DOWN THERE IN THE SHADOWS?
I WAS WAITING FOR YOU!
I CAME TO WARN YOU!

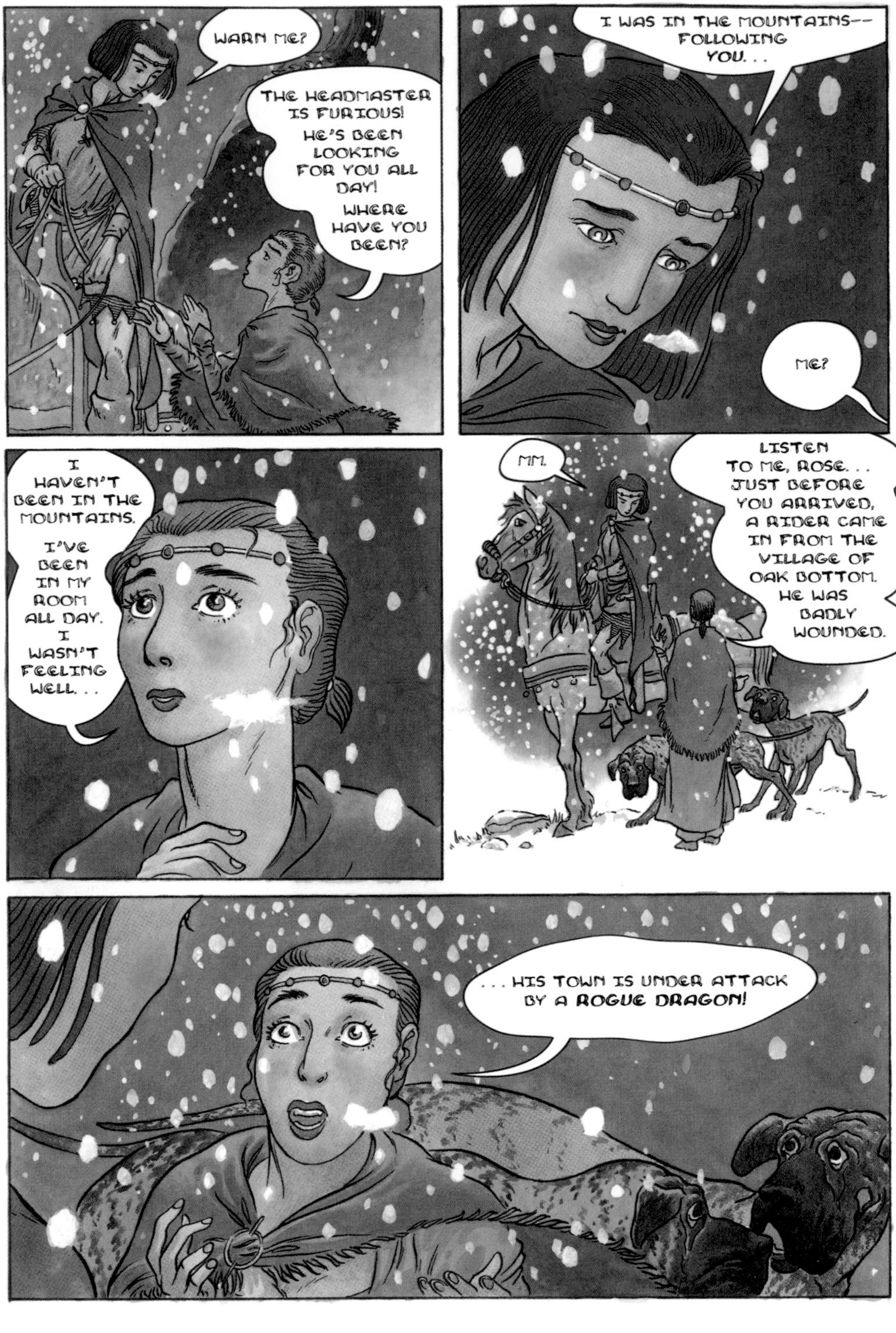
WARN ME?
THE HEADMASTER IS FURIOUS!
HE'S BEEN LOOKING FOR YOU ALL DAY!
WHERE HAVE YOU BEEN?
I WAS IN THE MOUNTAINS-- FOLLOWING YOU. . .
ME?
I HAVEN'T BEEN IN THE MOUNTAINS.
I'VE BEEN IN MY ROOM ALL DAY. I WASN'T FEELING WELL. . .
MM.
LISTEN TO ME, ROSE. . . JUST BEFORE YOU ARRIVED, A RIDER CAME IN FROM THE VILLAGE OF OAK BOTTOM. HE WAS BADLY WOUNDED.
. . . HIS TOWN IS UNDER ATTACK BY A **ROGUE DRAGON**!

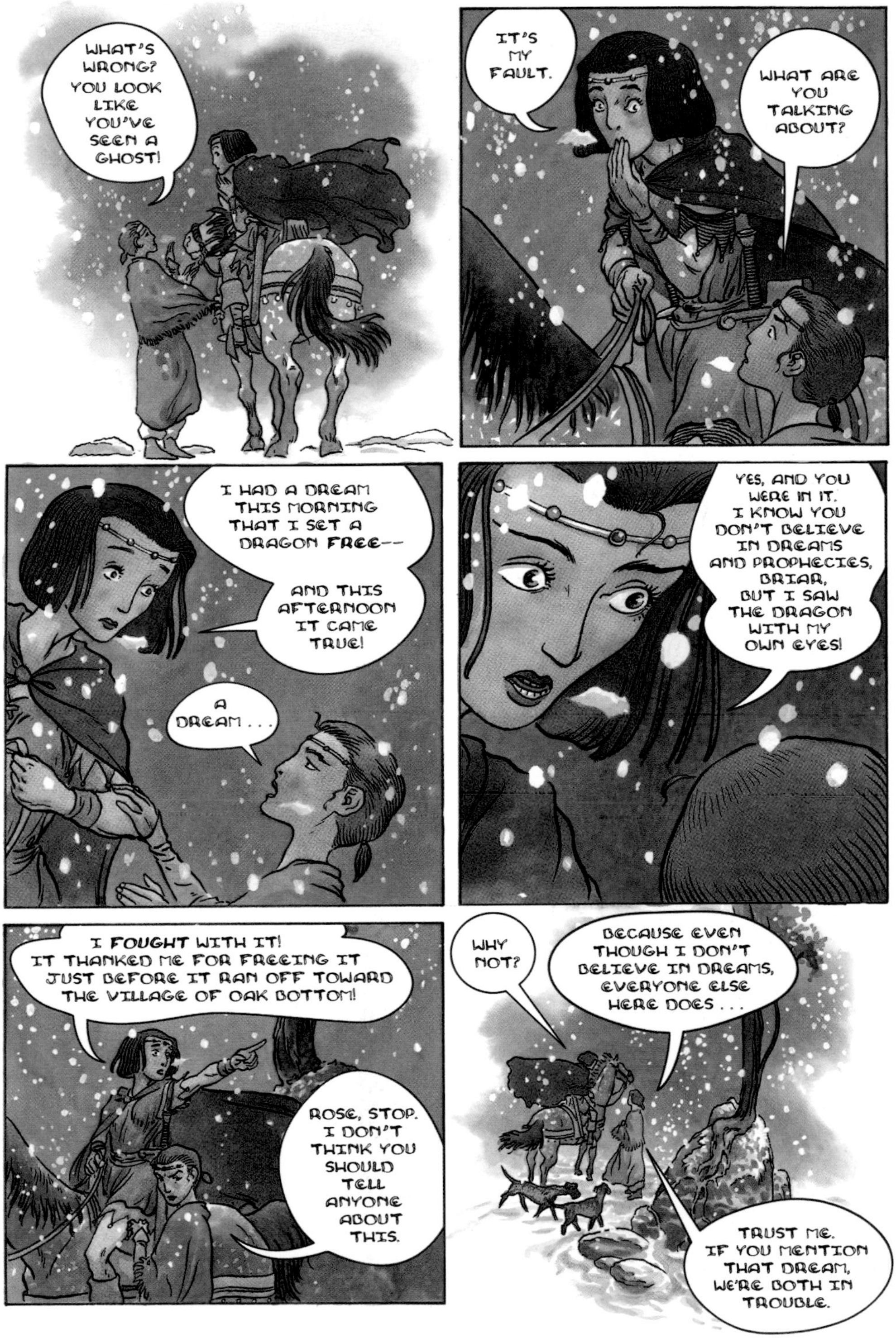
WHAT'S WRONG? YOU LOOK LIKE YOU'VE SEEN A GHOST!
IT'S MY FAULT.
WHAT ARE YOU TALKING ABOUT?
I HAD A DREAM THIS MORNING THAT I SET A DRAGON FREE--
AND THIS AFTERNOON IT CAME TRUE!
A DREAM . . .
YES, AND YOU WERE IN IT. I KNOW YOU DON'T BELIEVE IN DREAMS AND PROPHECIES, BRIAR, BUT I SAW THE DRAGON WITH MY OWN EYES!
I FOUGHT WITH IT! IT THANKED ME FOR FREEING IT JUST BEFORE IT RAN OFF TOWARD THE VILLAGE OF OAK BOTTOM!
ROSE, STOP. I DON'T THINK YOU SHOULD TELL ANYONE ABOUT THIS.
WHY NOT?
BECAUSE EVEN THOUGH I DON'T BELIEVE IN DREAMS, EVERYONE ELSE HERE DOES . . .
TRUST ME. IF YOU MENTION THAT DREAM, WE'RE BOTH IN TROUBLE.

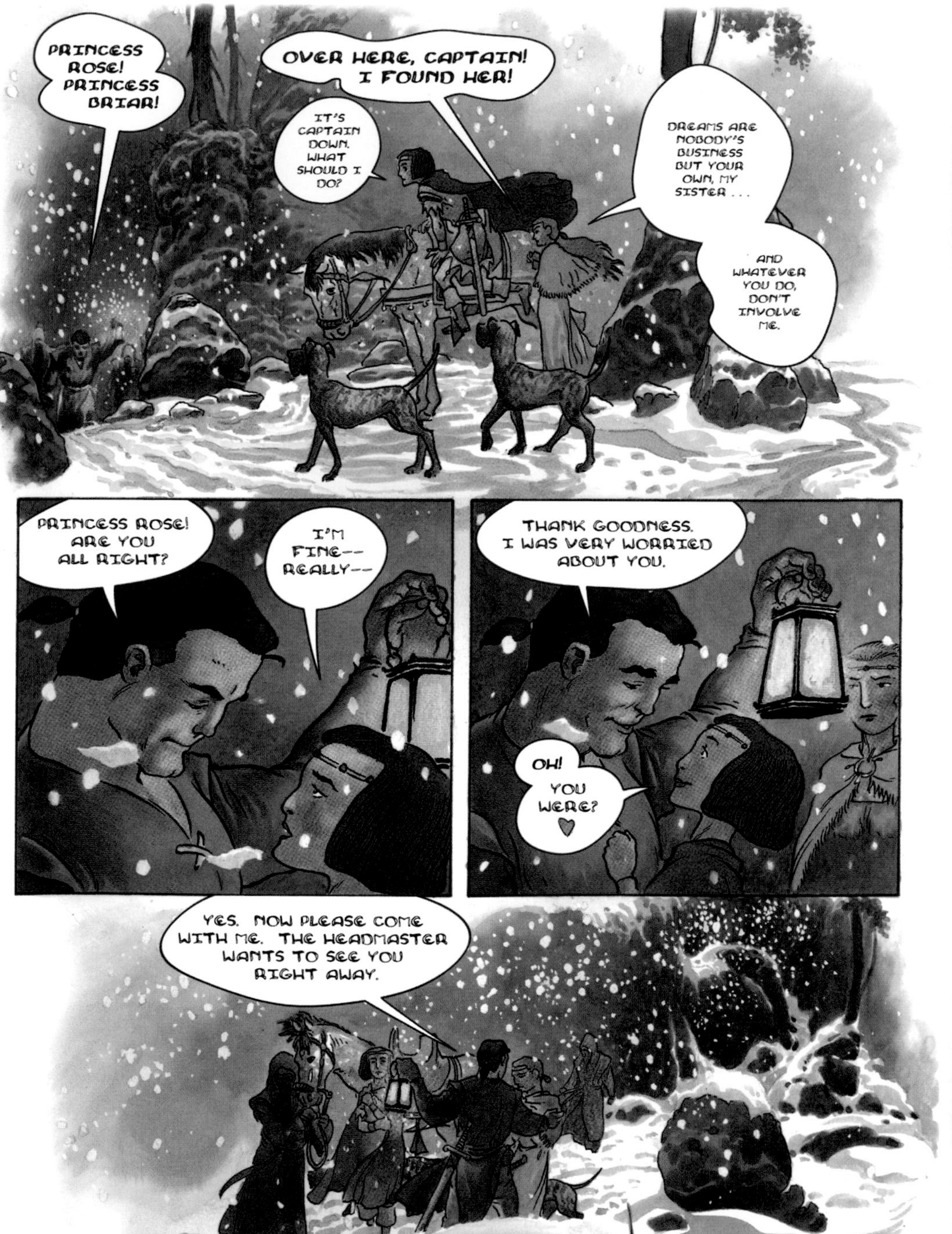
PRINCESS ROSE! PRINCESS BRIAR!
OVER HERE, CAPTAIN! I FOUND HER!
IT'S CAPTAIN DOWN. WHAT SHOULD I DO?
DREAMS ARE NOBODY'S BUSINESS BUT YOUR OWN, MY SISTER . . .
AND WHATEVER YOU DO, DON'T INVOLVE ME.
PRINCESS ROSE! ARE YOU ALL RIGHT?
I'M FINE-- REALLY--
THANK GOODNESS. I WAS VERY WORRIED ABOUT YOU.
OH! YOU WERE? ♥
YES. NOW PLEASE COME WITH ME. THE HEADMASTER WANTS TO SEE YOU RIGHT AWAY.

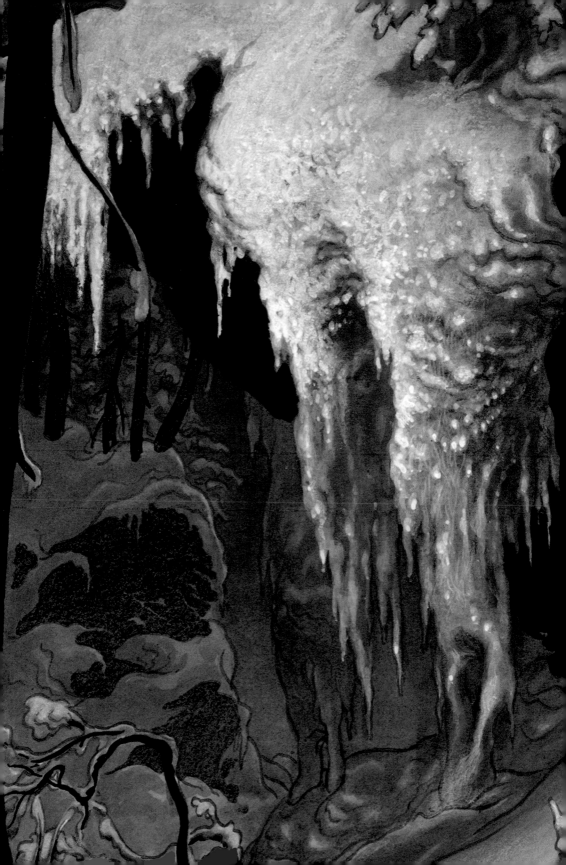

CHAPTER EIGHT

WH--
WHAT'S
GOING
ON?

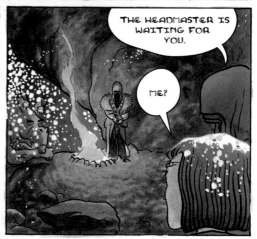

THE HEADMASTER IS
WAITING FOR
YOU.

ME?

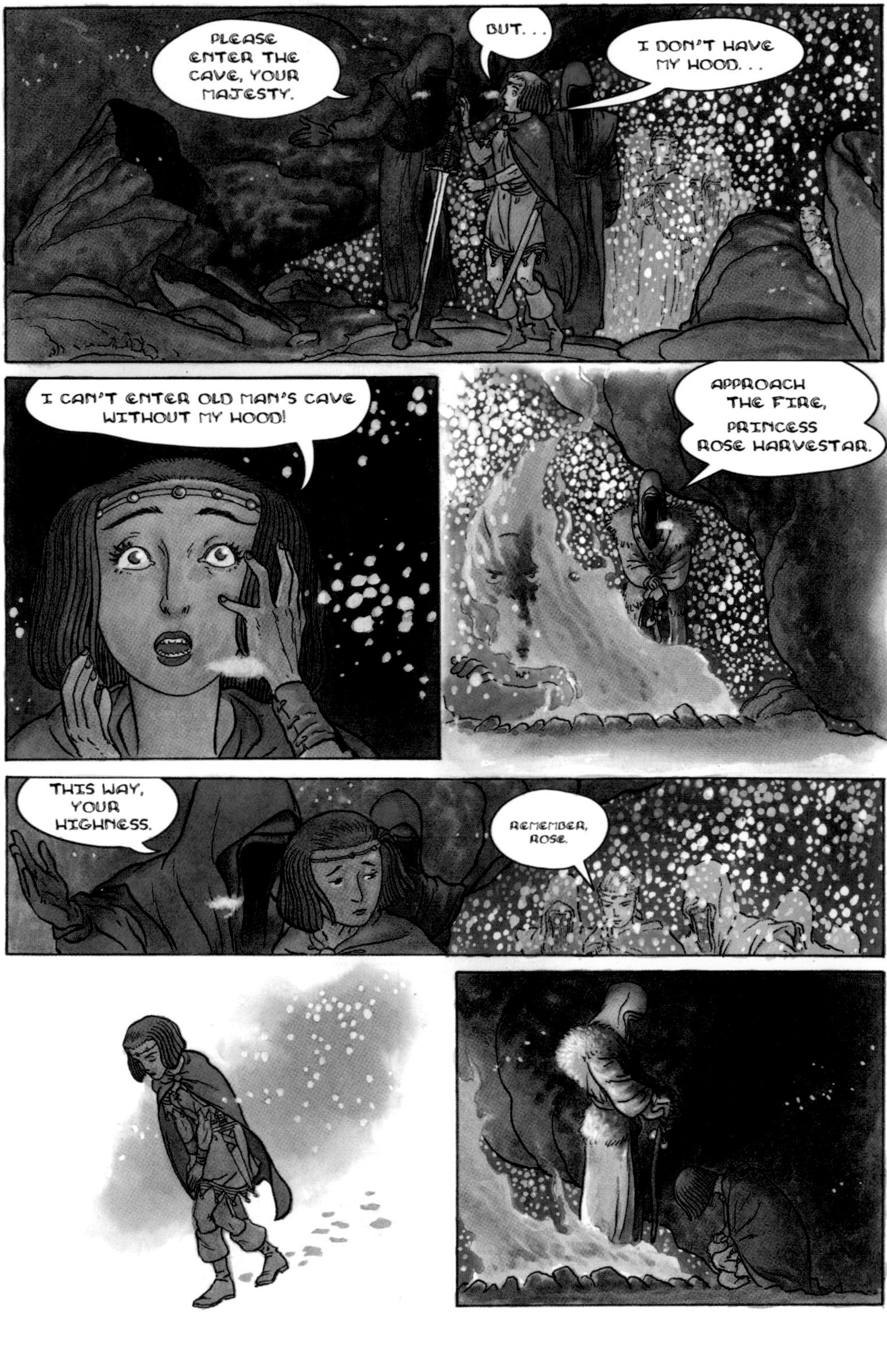
PLEASE ENTER THE CAVE, YOUR MAJESTY.
BUT. . .
I DON'T HAVE MY HOOD. . .
I CAN'T ENTER OLD MAN'S CAVE WITHOUT MY HOOD!
APPROACH THE FIRE, PRINCESS ROSE HARVESTAR.
THIS WAY, YOUR HIGHNESS.
REMEMBER, ROSE.

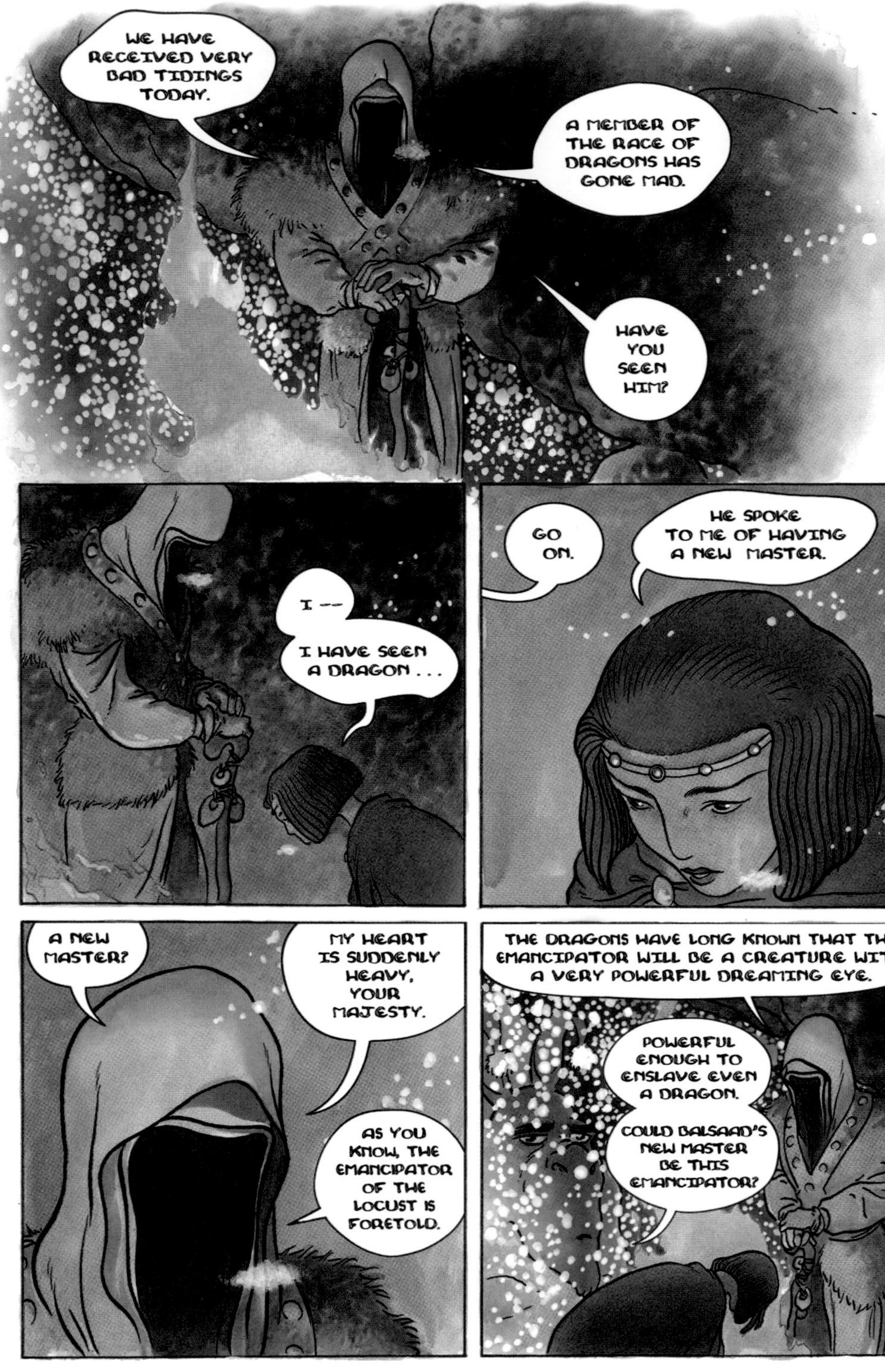
WE HAVE RECEIVED VERY BAD TIDINGS TODAY.
A MEMBER OF THE RACE OF DRAGONS HAS GONE MAD.
HAVE YOU SEEN HIM?
I --
I HAVE SEEN A DRAGON . . .
GO ON.
HE SPOKE TO ME OF HAVING A NEW MASTER.
A NEW MASTER?
MY HEART IS SUDDENLY HEAVY, YOUR MAJESTY.
AS YOU KNOW, THE EMANCIPATOR OF THE LOCUST IS FORETOLD.
THE DRAGONS HAVE LONG KNOWN THAT THE EMANCIPATOR WILL BE A CREATURE WITH A VERY POWERFUL DREAMING EYE.
POWERFUL ENOUGH TO ENSLAVE EVEN A DRAGON.
COULD BALSAAD'S NEW MASTER BE THIS EMANCIPATOR?

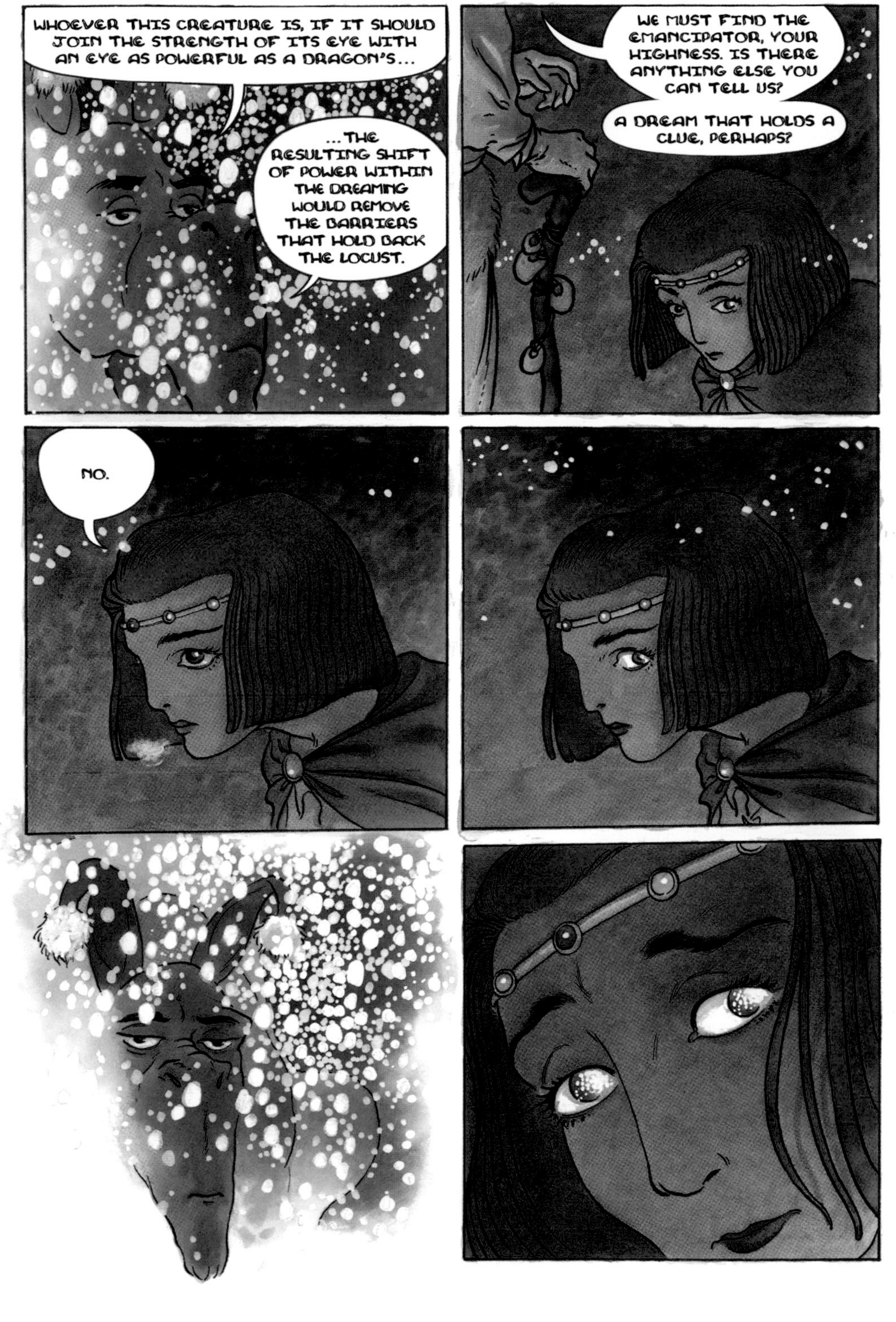
WHOEVER THIS CREATURE IS, IF IT SHOULD JOIN THE STRENGTH OF ITS EYE WITH AN EYE AS POWERFUL AS A DRAGON'S...
...THE RESULTING SHIFT OF POWER WITHIN THE DREAMING WOULD REMOVE THE BARRIERS THAT HOLD BACK THE LOCUST.
WE MUST FIND THE EMANCIPATOR, YOUR HIGHNESS. IS THERE ANYTHING ELSE YOU CAN TELL US?
A DREAM THAT HOLDS A CLUE, PERHAPS?
NO.

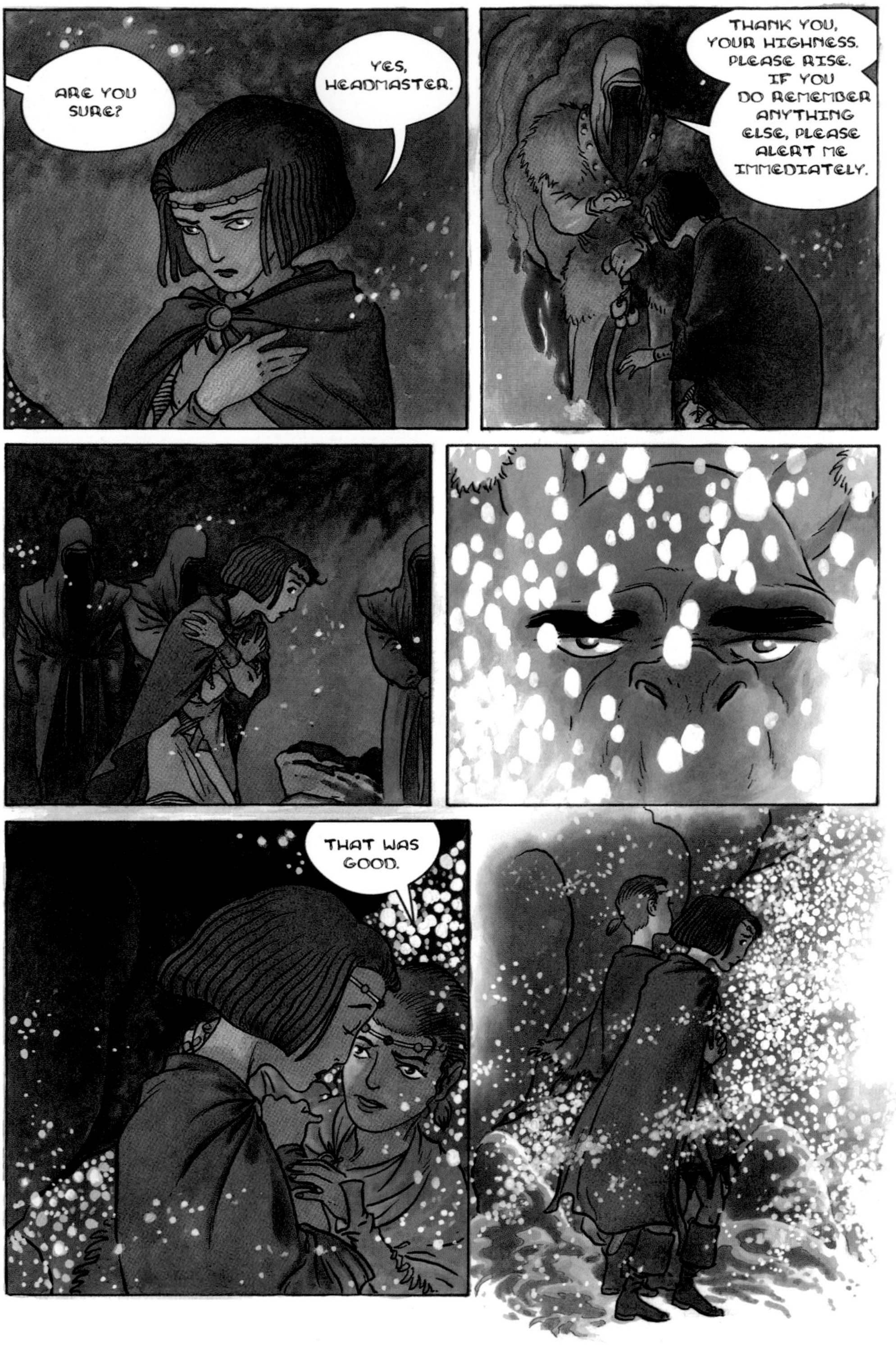
ARE YOU SURE?
YES, HEADMASTER.
THANK YOU, YOUR HIGHNESS. PLEASE RISE. IF YOU DO REMEMBER ANYTHING ELSE, PLEASE ALERT ME IMMEDIATELY.
THAT WAS GOOD.

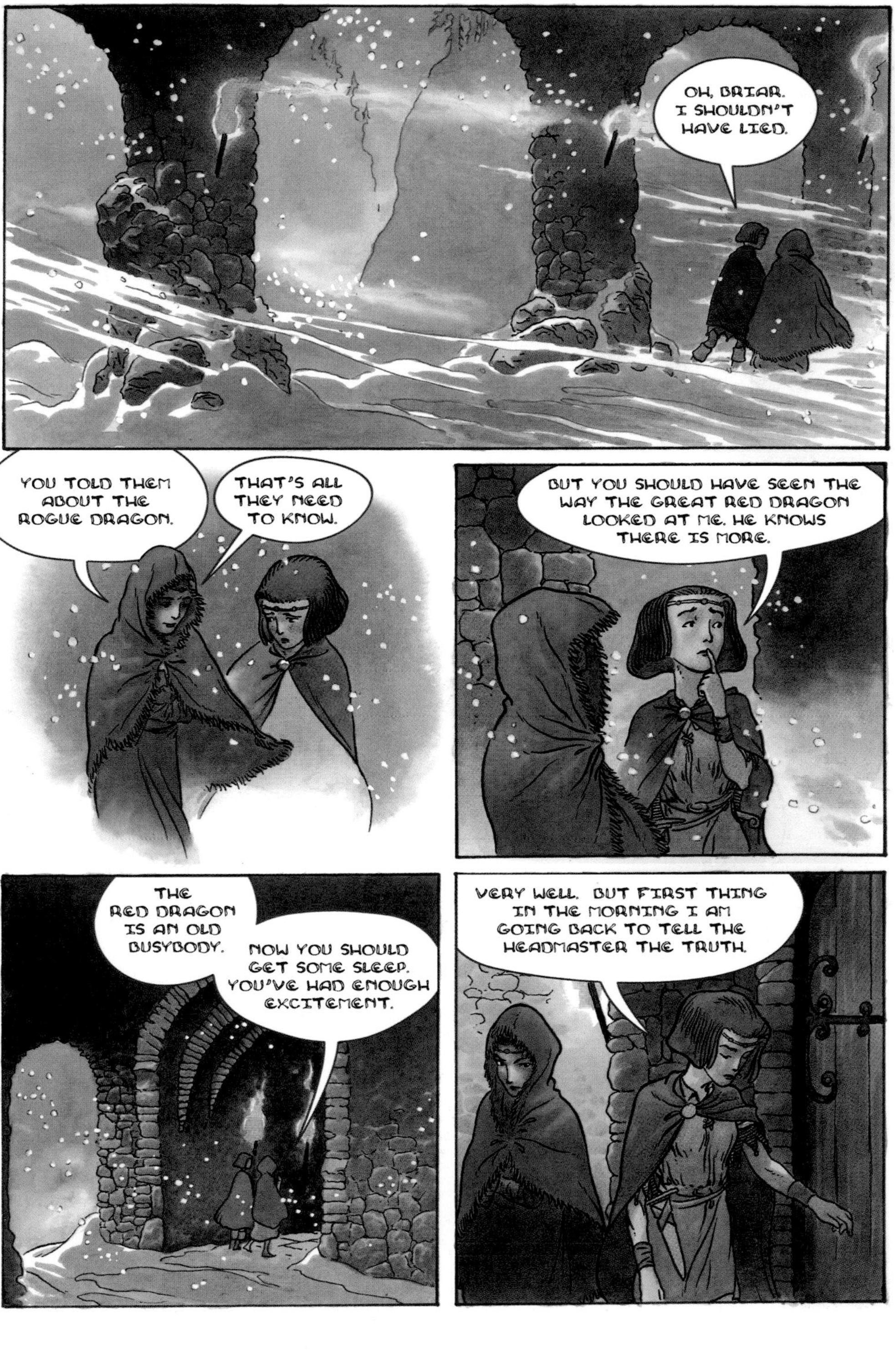
OH, BRIAR. I SHOULDN'T HAVE LIED.
YOU TOLD THEM ABOUT THE ROGUE DRAGON.
THAT'S ALL THEY NEED TO KNOW.
BUT YOU SHOULD HAVE SEEN THE WAY THE GREAT RED DRAGON LOOKED AT ME. HE KNOWS THERE IS MORE.
THE RED DRAGON IS AN OLD BUSYBODY.
NOW YOU SHOULD GET SOME SLEEP. YOU'VE HAD ENOUGH EXCITEMENT.
VERY WELL. BUT FIRST THING IN THE MORNING I AM GOING BACK TO TELL THE HEADMASTER THE TRUTH.

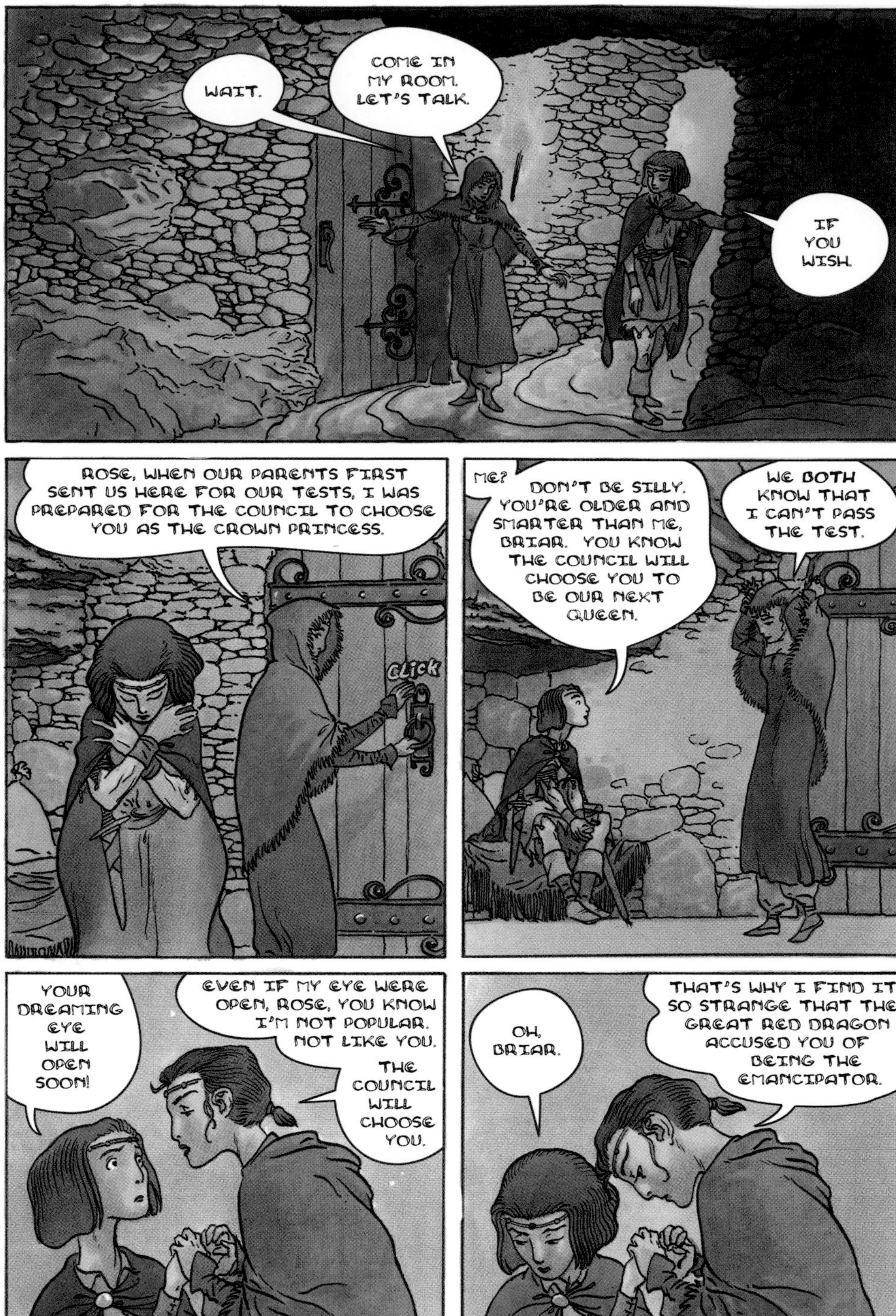
WAIT.
COME IN MY ROOM. LET'S TALK.
IF YOU WISH.
ROSE, WHEN OUR PARENTS FIRST SENT US HERE FOR OUR TESTS, I WAS PREPARED FOR THE COUNCIL TO CHOOSE YOU AS THE CROWN PRINCESS.
CLICK
ME?
DON'T BE SILLY. YOU'RE OLDER AND SMARTER THAN ME, BRIAR. YOU KNOW THE COUNCIL WILL CHOOSE YOU TO BE OUR NEXT QUEEN.
WE BOTH KNOW THAT I CAN'T PASS THE TEST.
YOUR DREAMING EYE WILL OPEN SOON!
EVEN IF MY EYE WERE OPEN, ROSE, YOU KNOW I'M NOT POPULAR. NOT LIKE YOU.
THE COUNCIL WILL CHOOSE YOU.
OH, BRIAR.
THAT'S WHY I FIND IT SO STRANGE THAT THE GREAT RED DRAGON ACCUSED YOU OF BEING THE EMANCIPATOR.

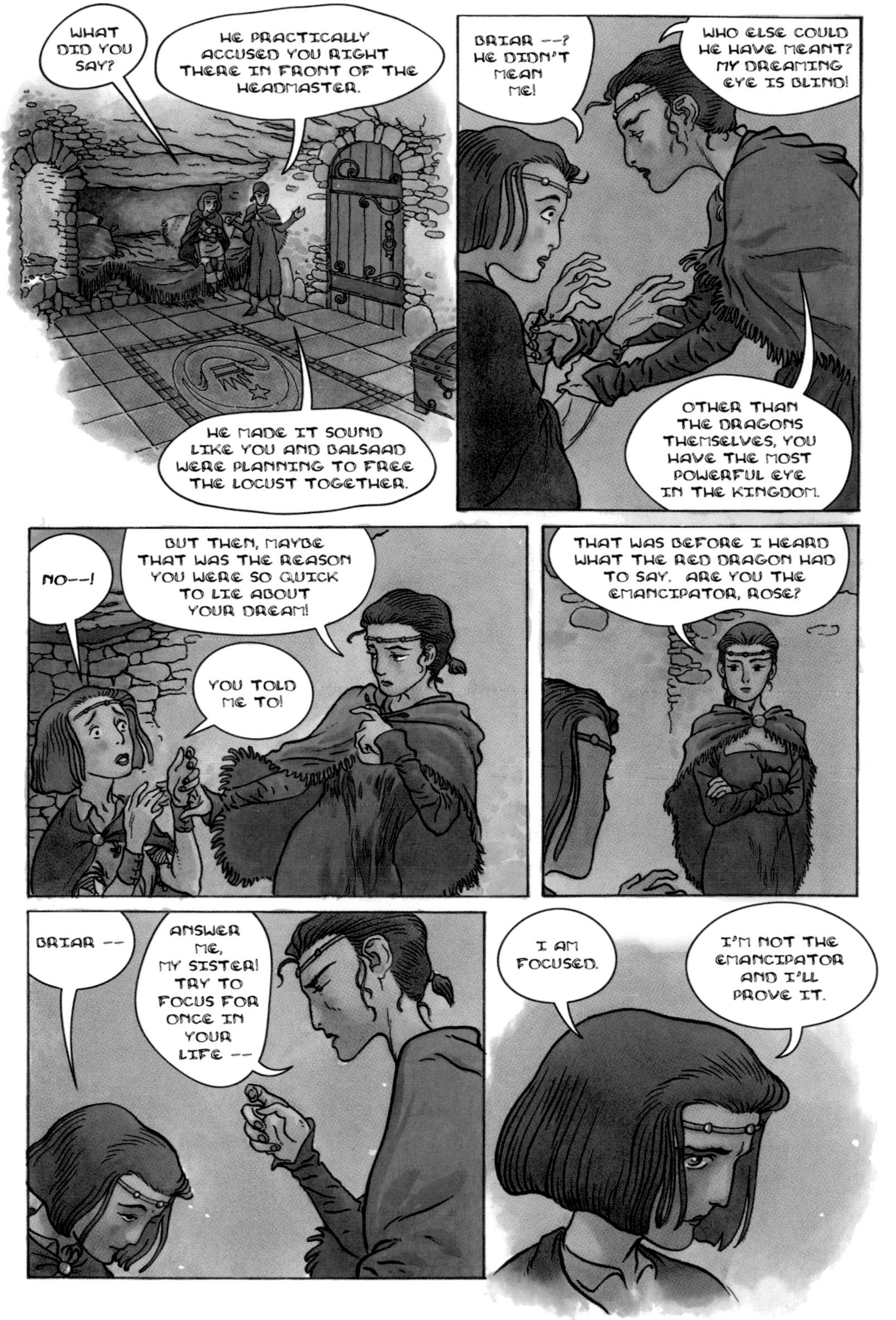
WHAT DID YOU SAY?
HE PRACTICALLY ACCUSED YOU RIGHT THERE IN FRONT OF THE HEADMASTER.
HE MADE IT SOUND LIKE YOU AND BALSAAD WERE PLANNING TO FREE THE LOCUST TOGETHER.
BRIAR --? HE DIDN'T MEAN ME!
WHO ELSE COULD HE HAVE MEANT? MY DREAMING EYE IS BLIND!
OTHER THAN THE DRAGONS THEMSELVES, YOU HAVE THE MOST POWERFUL EYE IN THE KINGDOM.
NO--!
BUT THEN, MAYBE THAT WAS THE REASON YOU WERE SO QUICK TO LIE ABOUT YOUR DREAM!
YOU TOLD ME TO!
THAT WAS BEFORE I HEARD WHAT THE RED DRAGON HAD TO SAY. ARE YOU THE EMANCIPATOR, ROSE?
BRIAR --
ANSWER ME, MY SISTER! TRY TO FOCUS FOR ONCE IN YOUR LIFE --
I AM FOCUSED.
I'M NOT THE EMANCIPATOR AND I'LL PROVE IT.

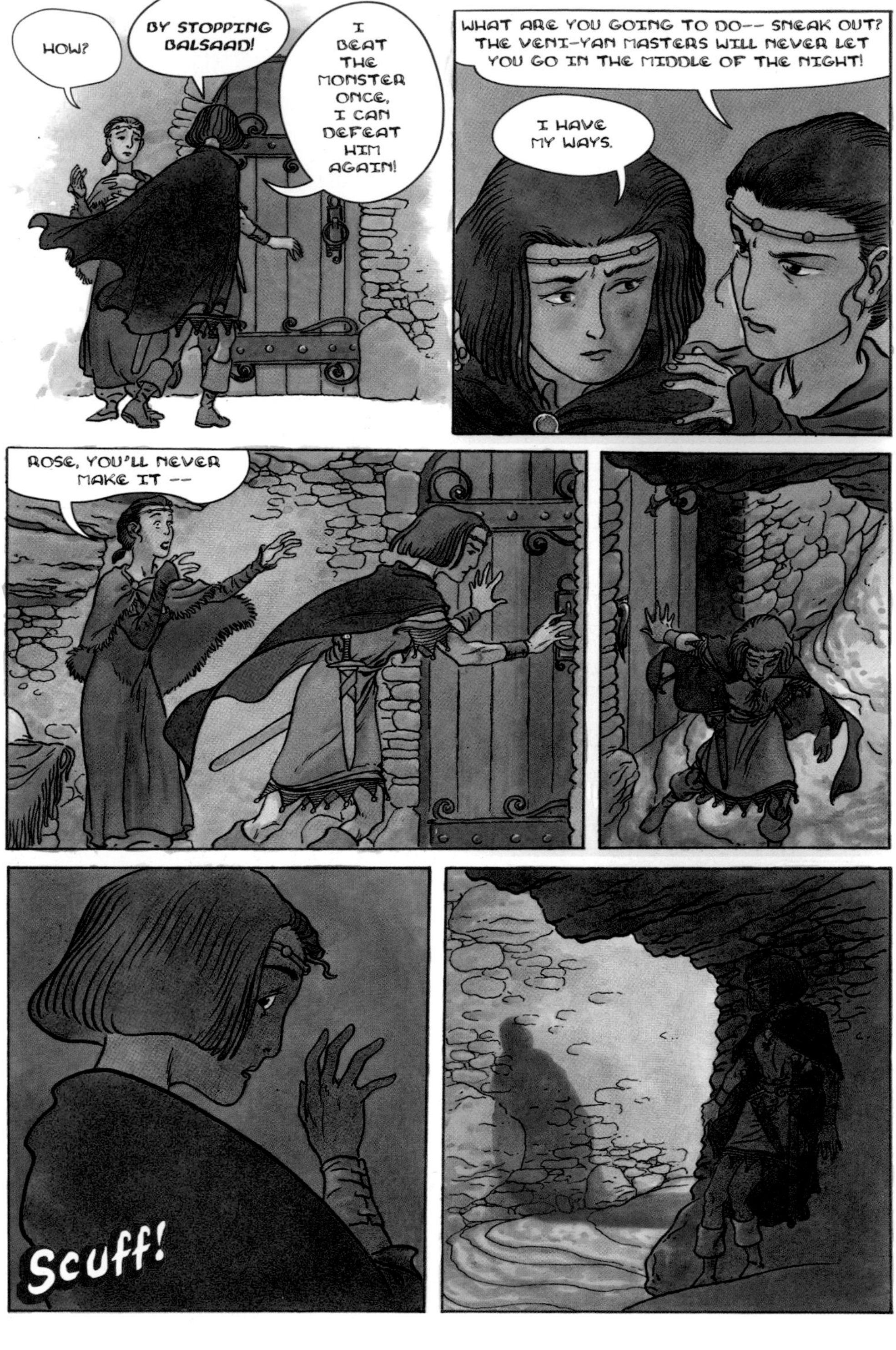
HOW?
BY STOPPING BALSAAD!
I BEAT THE MONSTER ONCE, I CAN DEFEAT HIM AGAIN!
WHAT ARE YOU GOING TO DO-- SNEAK OUT? THE VENI-YAN MASTERS WILL NEVER LET YOU GO IN THE MIDDLE OF THE NIGHT!
I HAVE MY WAYS.
ROSE, YOU'LL NEVER MAKE IT --
Scuff!

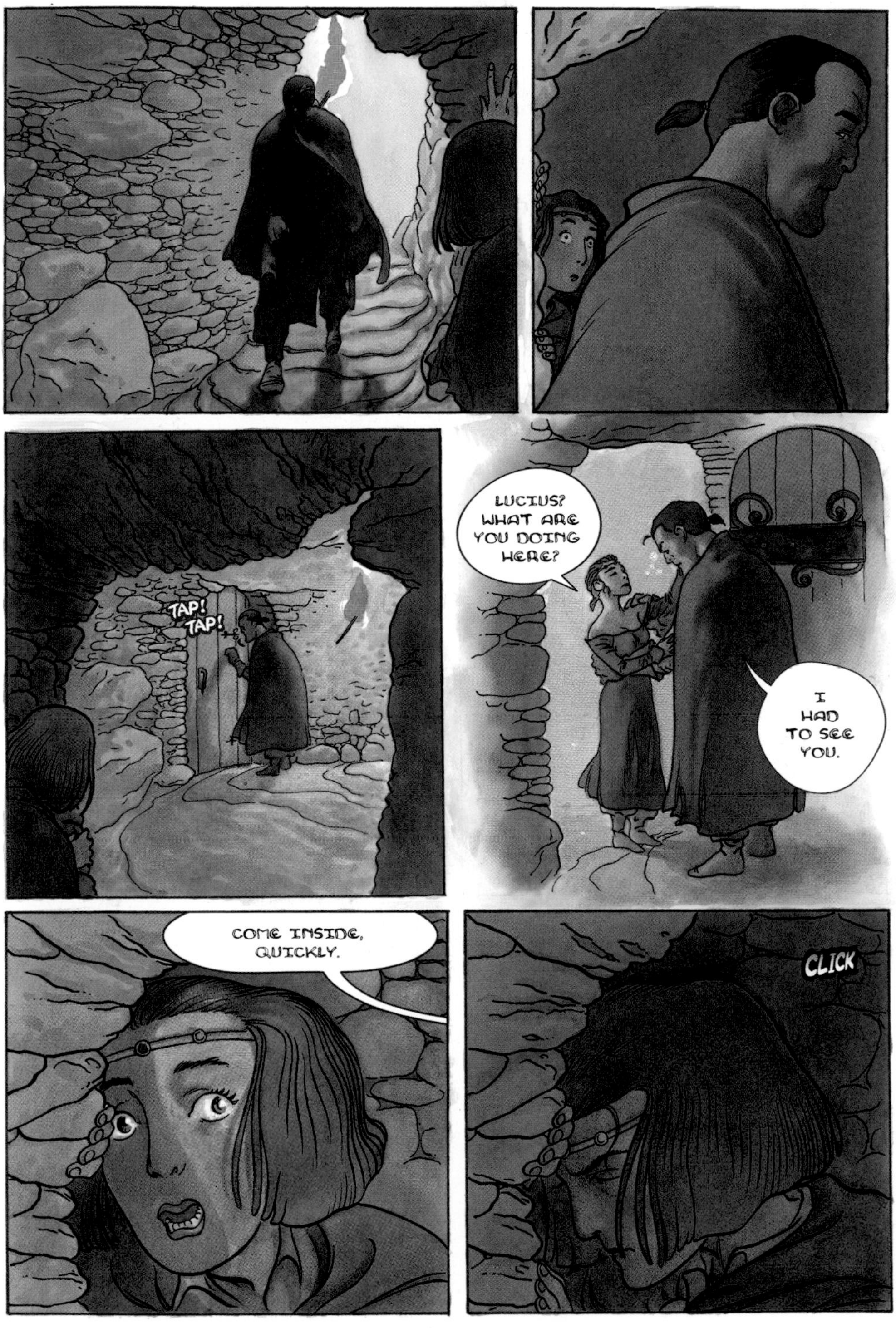
TAP!
TAP!
LUCIUS? WHAT ARE YOU DOING HERE?
I HAD TO SEE YOU.
COME INSIDE, QUICKLY.
CLICK

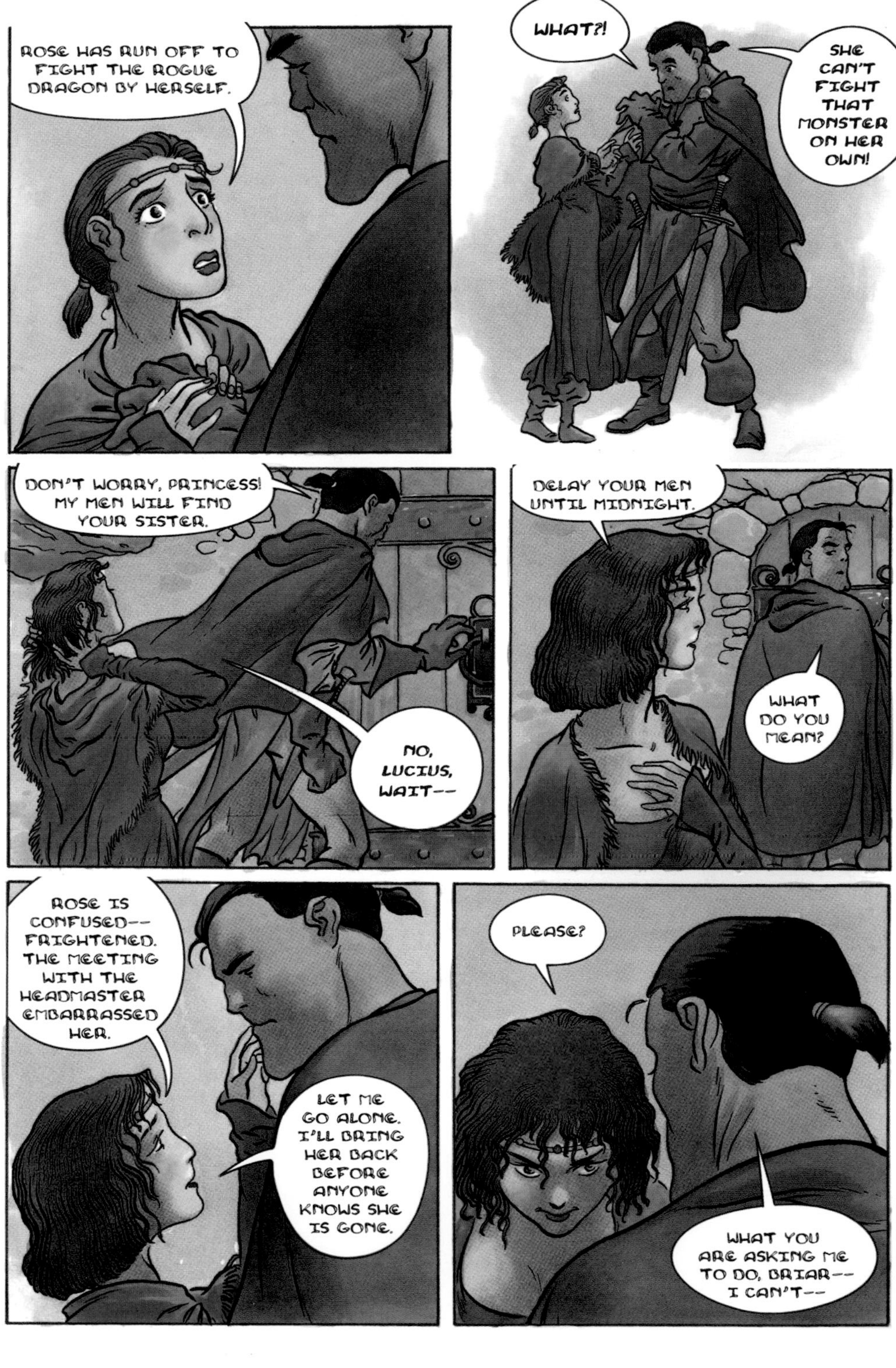
ROSE HAS RUN OFF TO FIGHT THE ROGUE DRAGON BY HERSELF.
WHAT?!
SHE CAN'T FIGHT THAT MONSTER ON HER OWN!
DON'T WORRY, PRINCESS! MY MEN WILL FIND YOUR SISTER.
NO, LUCIUS, WAIT--
DELAY YOUR MEN UNTIL MIDNIGHT.
WHAT DO YOU MEAN?
ROSE IS CONFUSED-- FRIGHTENED. THE MEETING WITH THE HEADMASTER EMBARRASSED HER.
LET ME GO ALONE. I'LL BRING HER BACK BEFORE ANYONE KNOWS SHE IS GONE.
PLEASE?
WHAT YOU ARE ASKING ME TO DO, BRIAR-- I CAN'T--

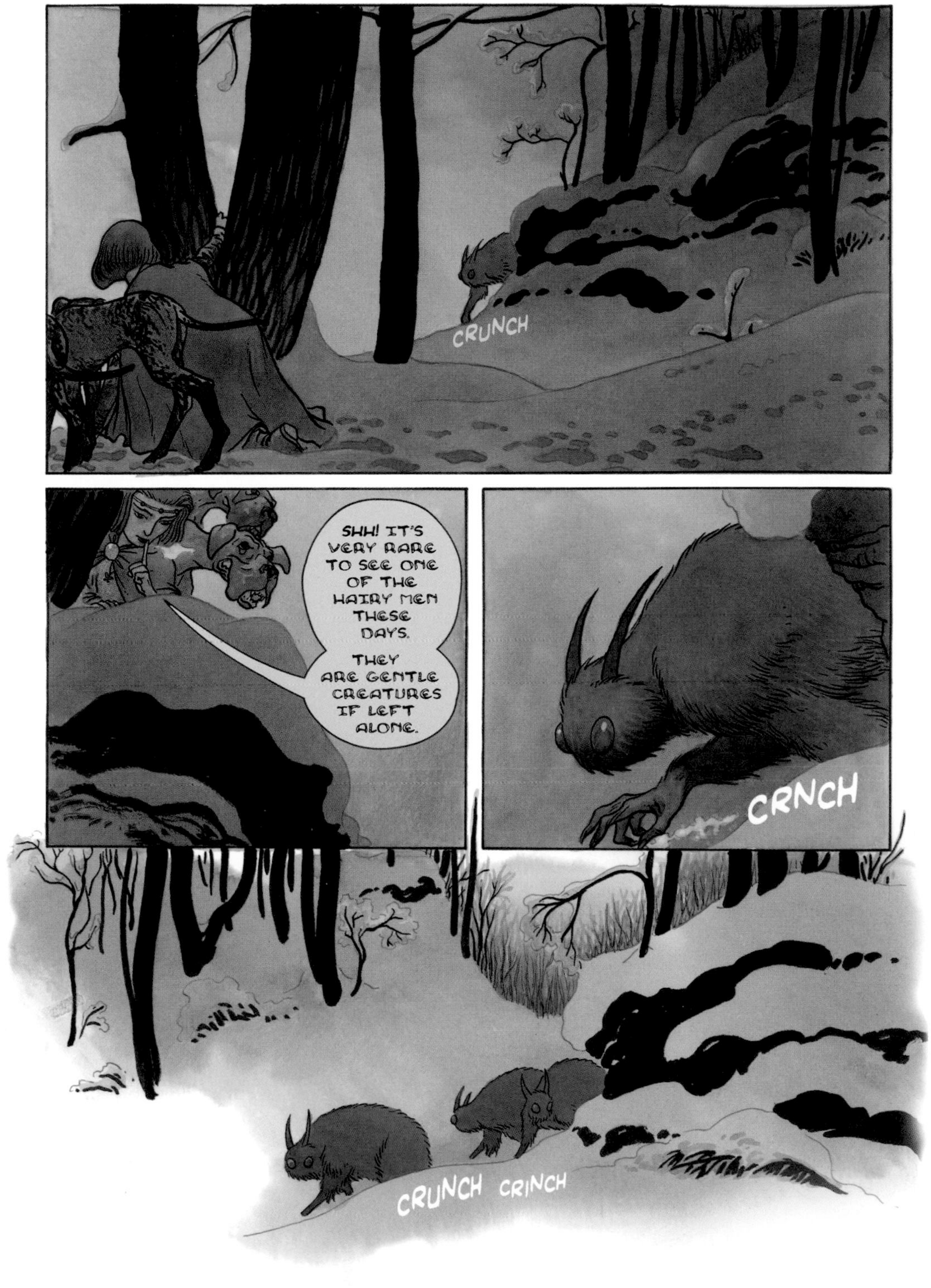
CRUNCH
SHH! IT'S VERY RARE TO SEE ONE OF THE HAIRY MEN THESE DAYS.
THEY ARE GENTLE CREATURES IF LEFT ALONE.
CRNCH
CRUNCH CRINCH

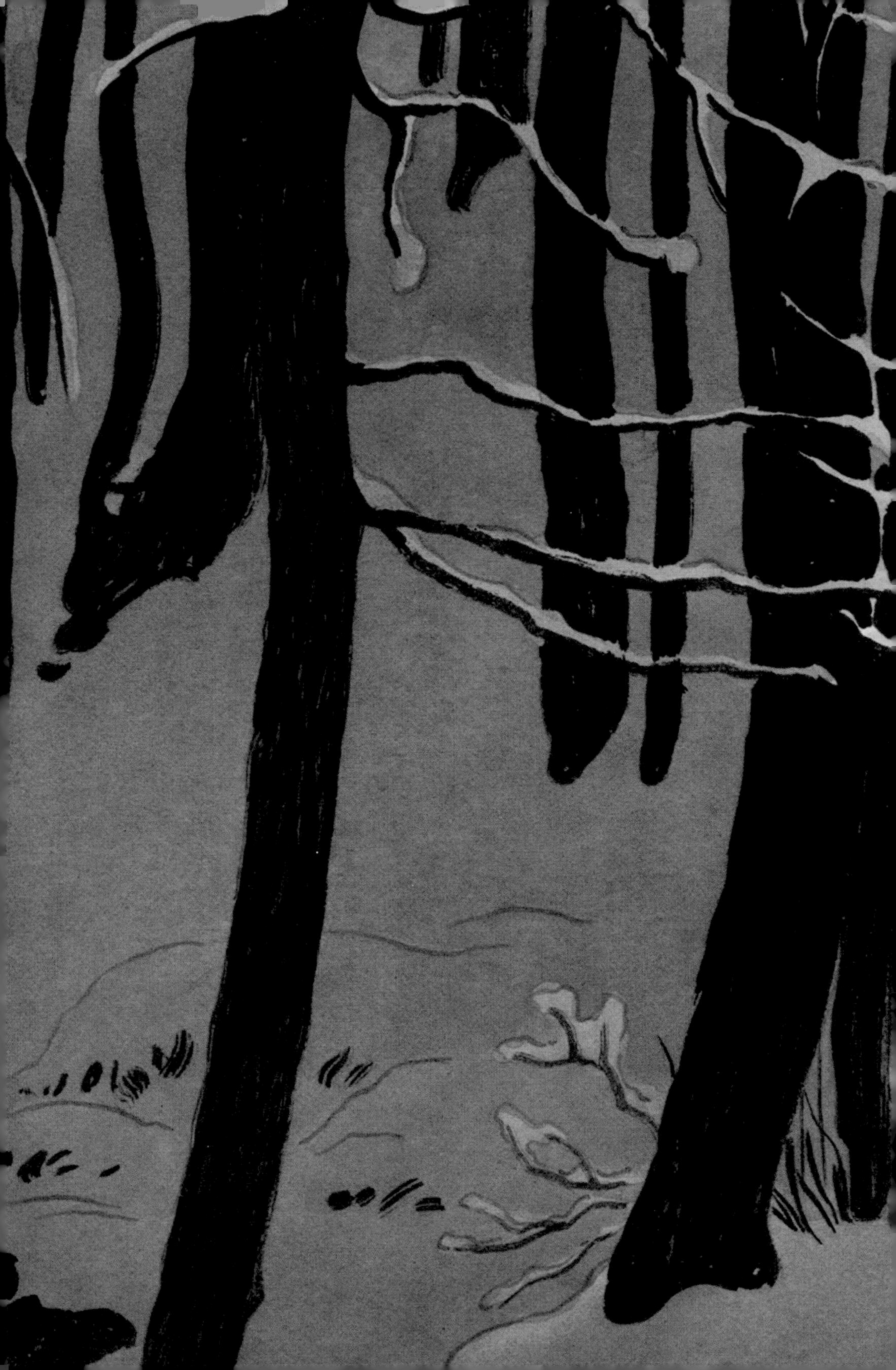

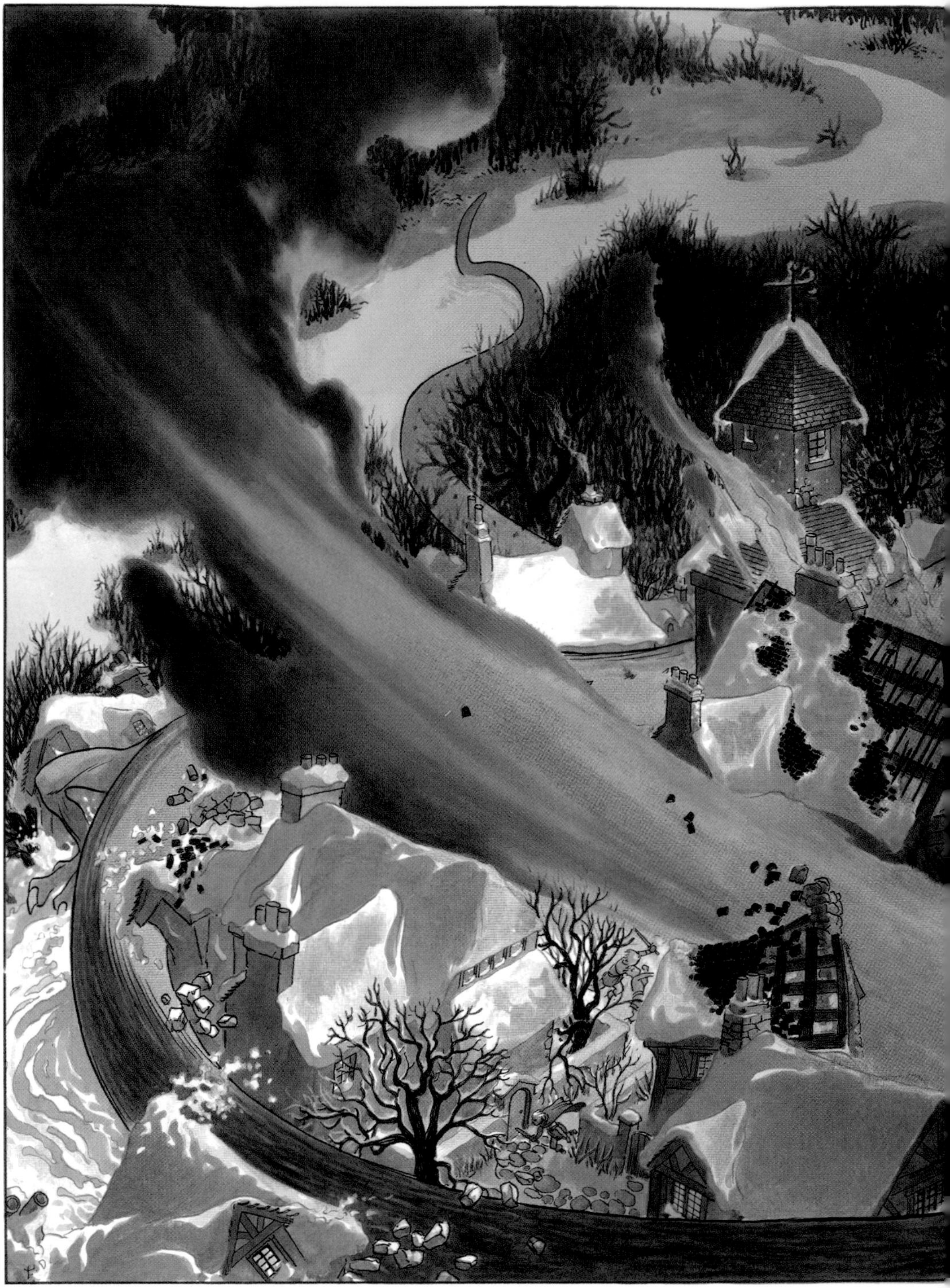

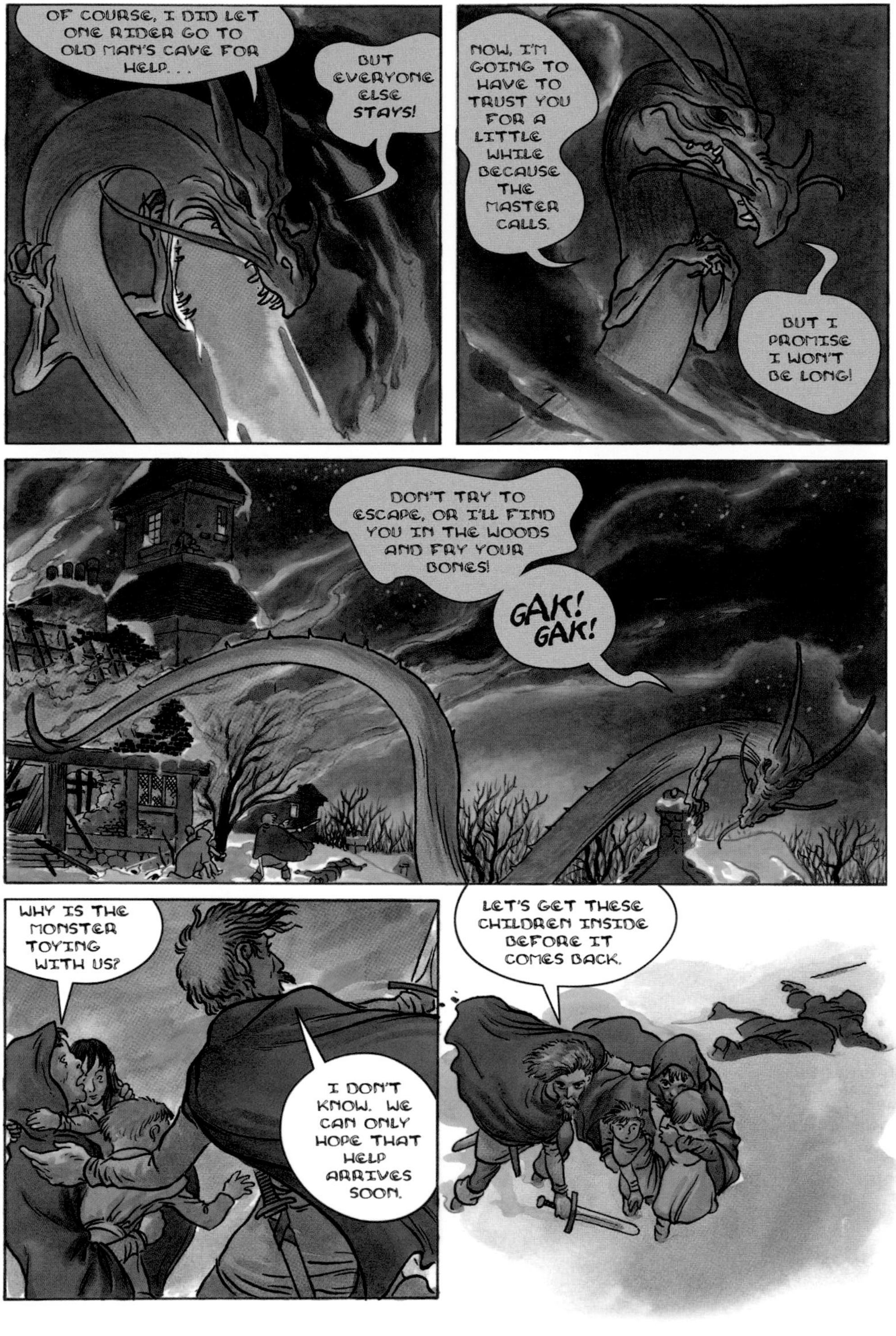
OF COURSE, I DID LET ONE RIDER GO TO OLD MAN'S CAVE FOR HELP. . .
BUT EVERYONE ELSE STAYS!
NOW, I'M GOING TO HAVE TO TRUST YOU FOR A LITTLE WHILE BECAUSE THE MASTER CALLS.
BUT I PROMISE I WON'T BE LONG!
DON'T TRY TO ESCAPE, OR I'LL FIND YOU IN THE WOODS AND FRY YOUR BONES!
GAK! GAK!
WHY IS THE MONSTER TOYING WITH US?
I DON'T KNOW. WE CAN ONLY HOPE THAT HELP ARRIVES SOON.
LET'S GET THESE CHILDREN INSIDE BEFORE IT COMES BACK.

THE PACT

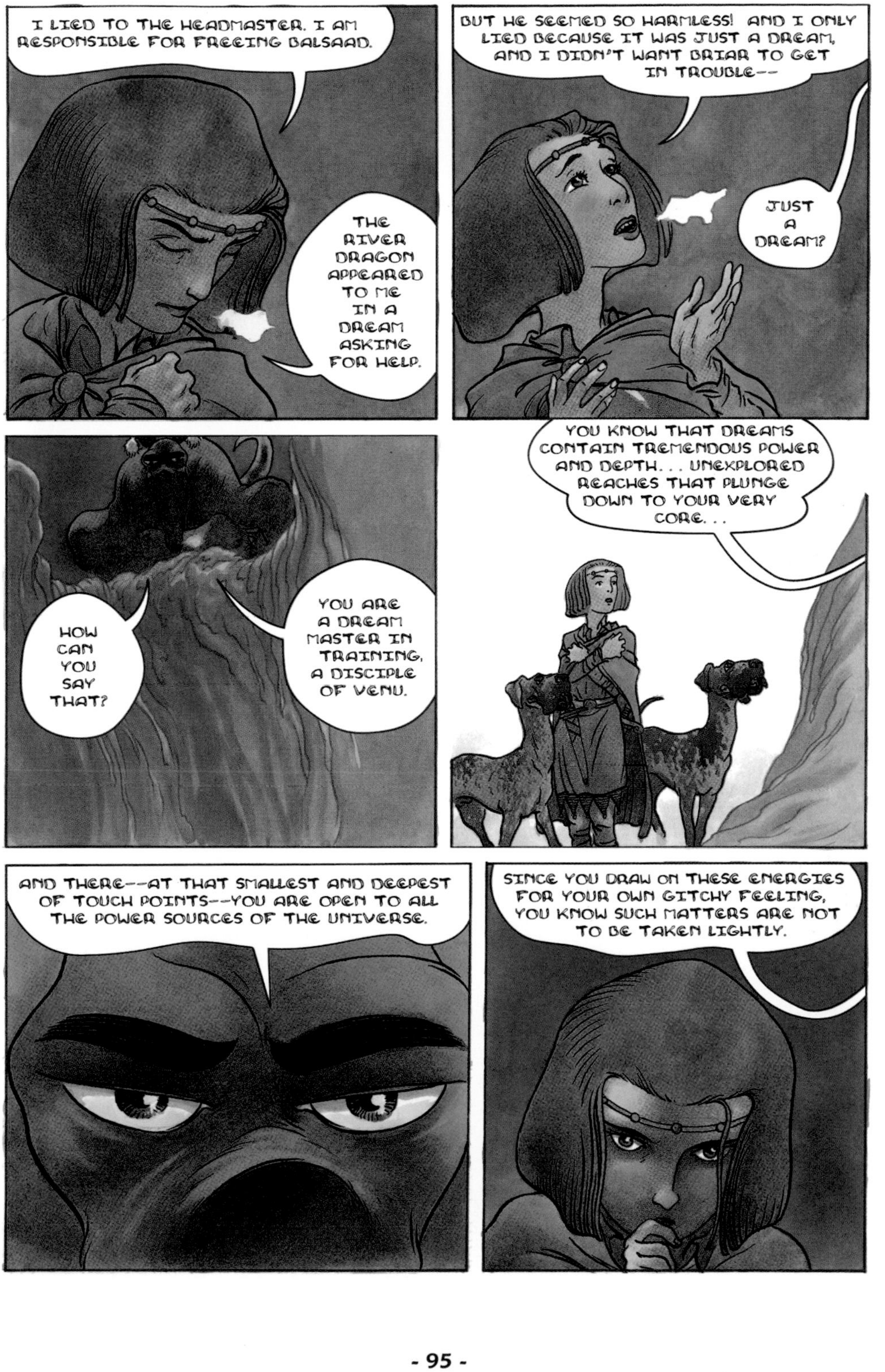
I LIED TO THE HEADMASTER. I AM RESPONSIBLE FOR FREEING BALSAAD.
THE RIVER DRAGON APPEARED TO ME IN A DREAM ASKING FOR HELP.
BUT HE SEEMED SO HARMLESS! AND I ONLY LIED BECAUSE IT WAS JUST A DREAM, AND I DIDN'T WANT BRIAR TO GET IN TROUBLE--
JUST A DREAM?
HOW CAN YOU SAY THAT?
YOU ARE A DREAM MASTER IN TRAINING, A DISCIPLE OF VENU.
YOU KNOW THAT DREAMS CONTAIN TREMENDOUS POWER AND DEPTH. . . UNEXPLORED REACHES THAT PLUNGE DOWN TO YOUR VERY CORE. . .
AND THERE--AT THAT SMALLEST AND DEEPEST OF TOUCH POINTS--YOU ARE OPEN TO ALL THE POWER SOURCES OF THE UNIVERSE.
SINCE YOU DRAW ON THESE ENERGIES FOR YOUR OWN GITCHY FEELING, YOU KNOW SUCH MATTERS ARE NOT TO BE TAKEN LIGHTLY.

FROZEN

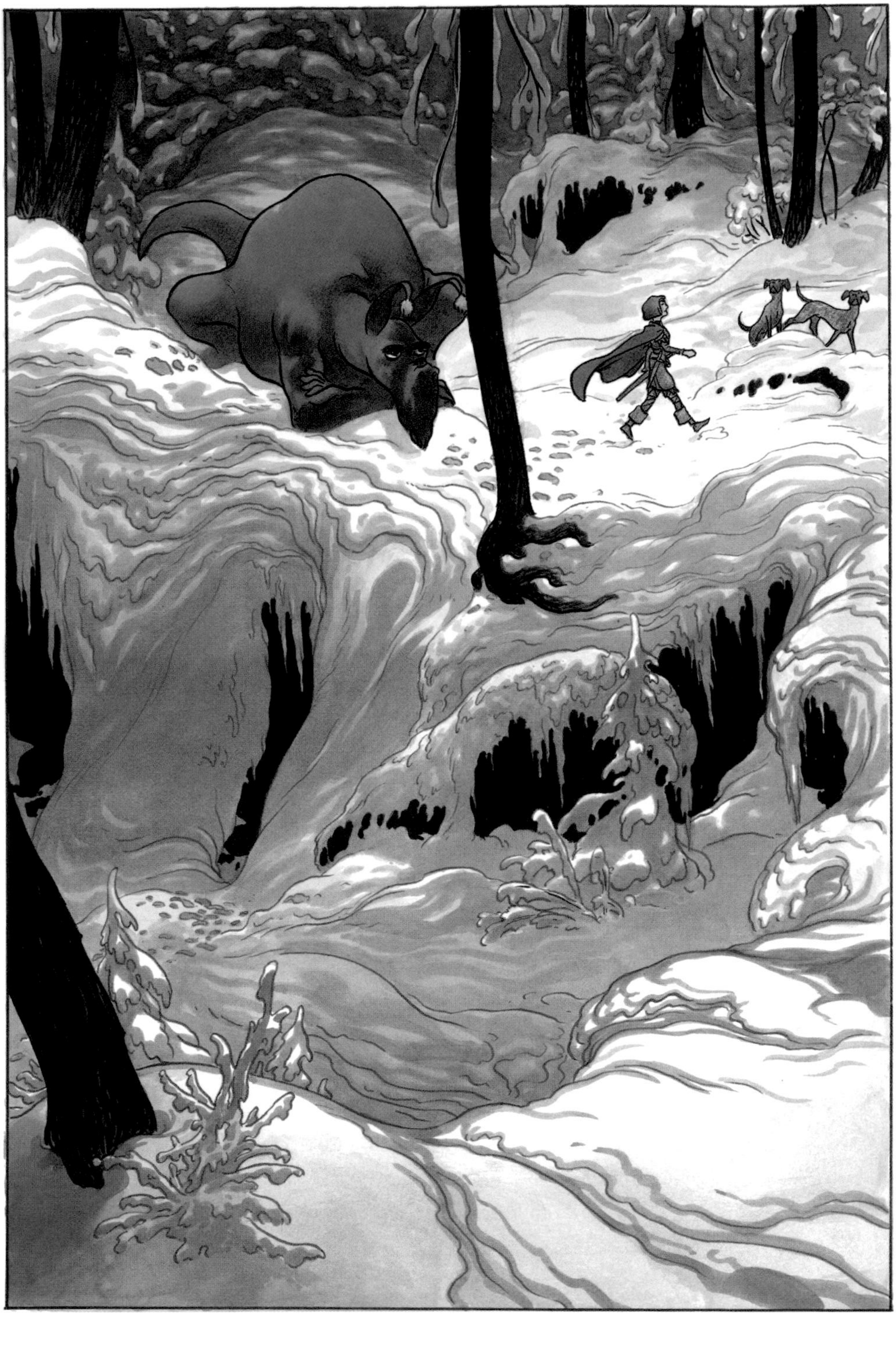

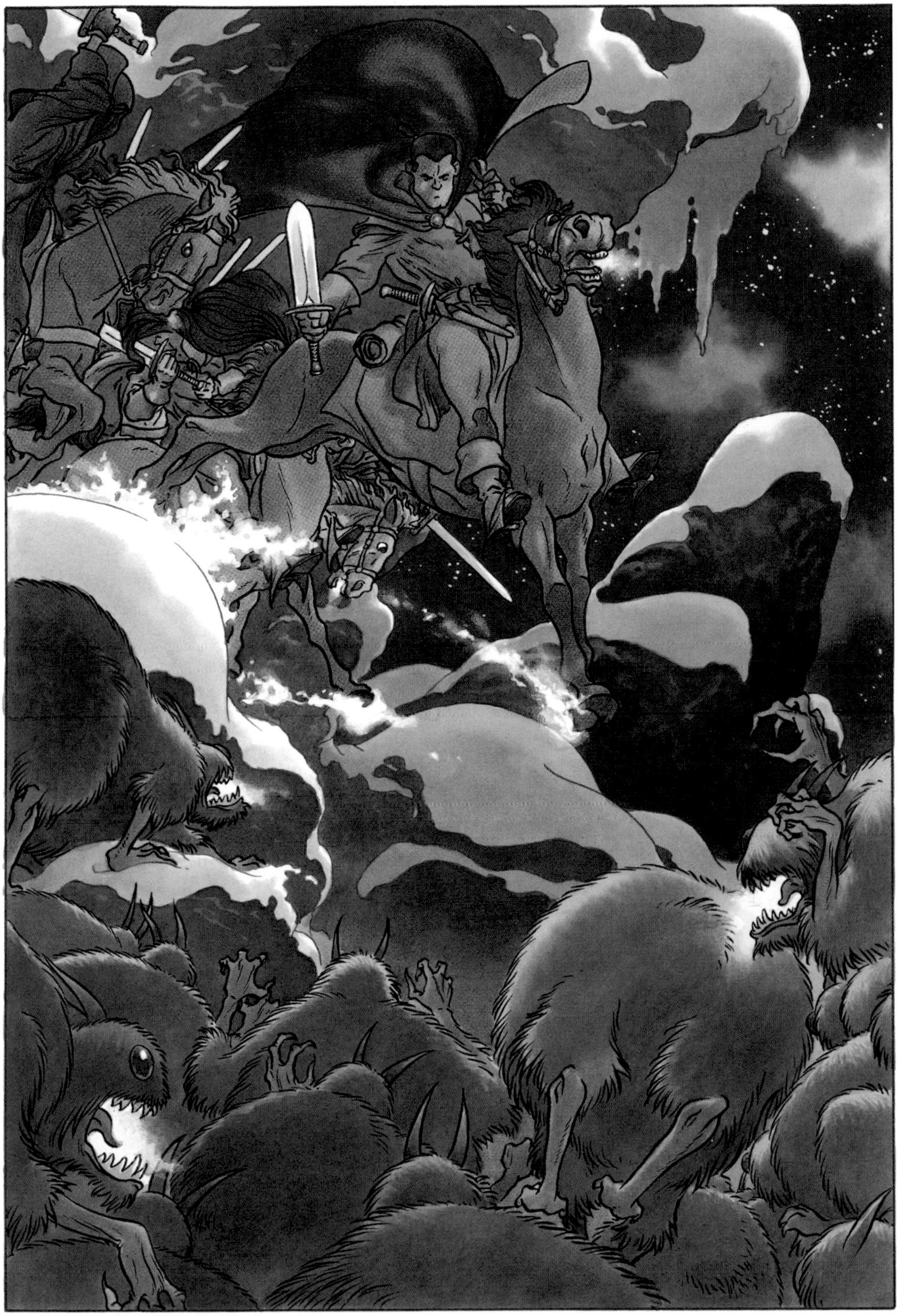

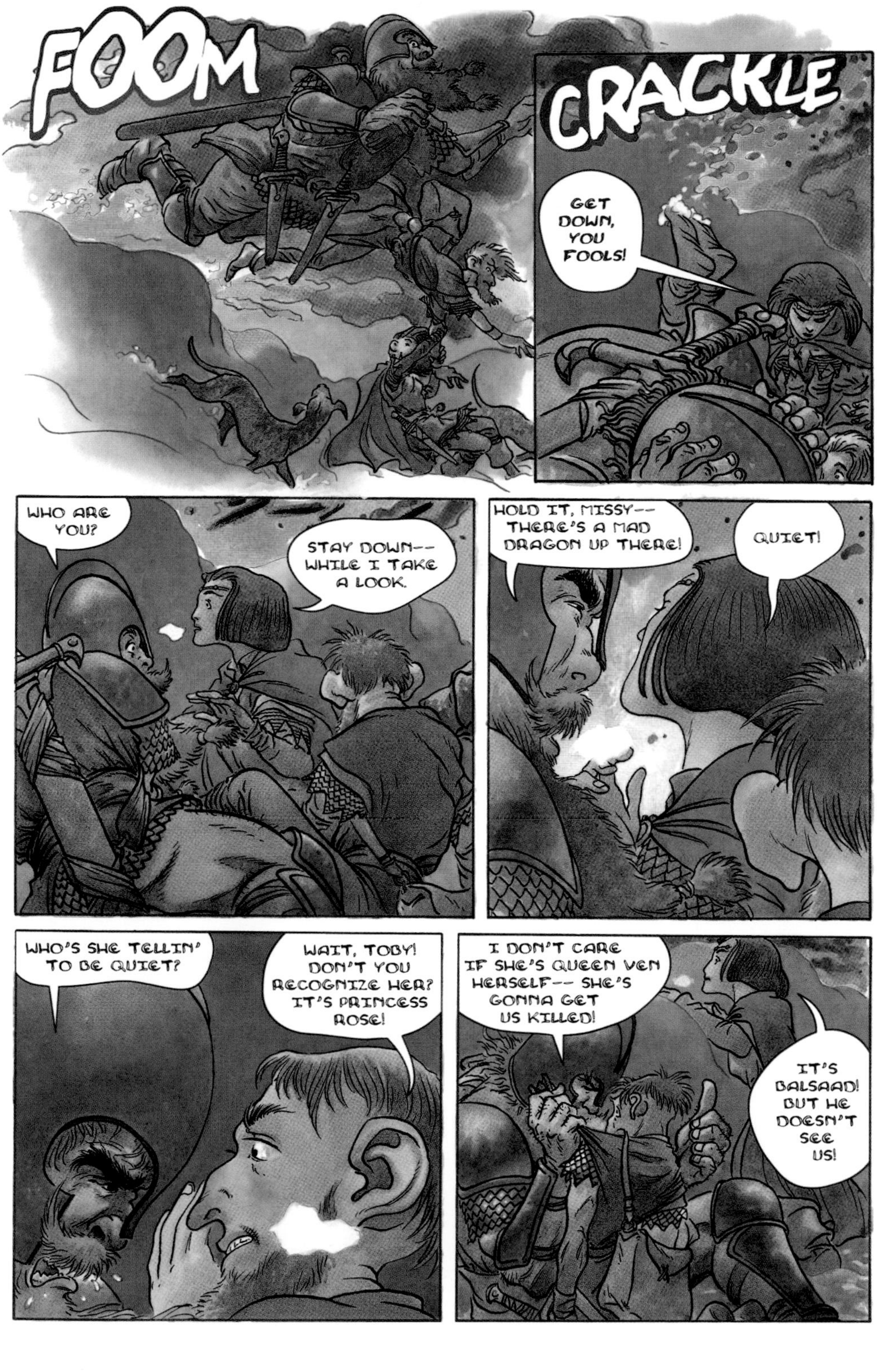
FOOM
CRACKLE
GET DOWN, YOU FOOLS!
WHO ARE YOU?
STAY DOWN-- WHILE I TAKE A LOOK.
HOLD IT, MISSY-- THERE'S A MAD DRAGON UP THERE!
QUIET!
WHO'S SHE TELLIN' TO BE QUIET?
WAIT, TOBY! DON'T YOU RECOGNIZE HER? IT'S PRINCESS ROSE!
I DON'T CARE IF SHE'S QUEEN VEN HERSELF-- SHE'S GONNA GET US KILLED!
IT'S BALSAAD! BUT HE DOESN'T SEE US!

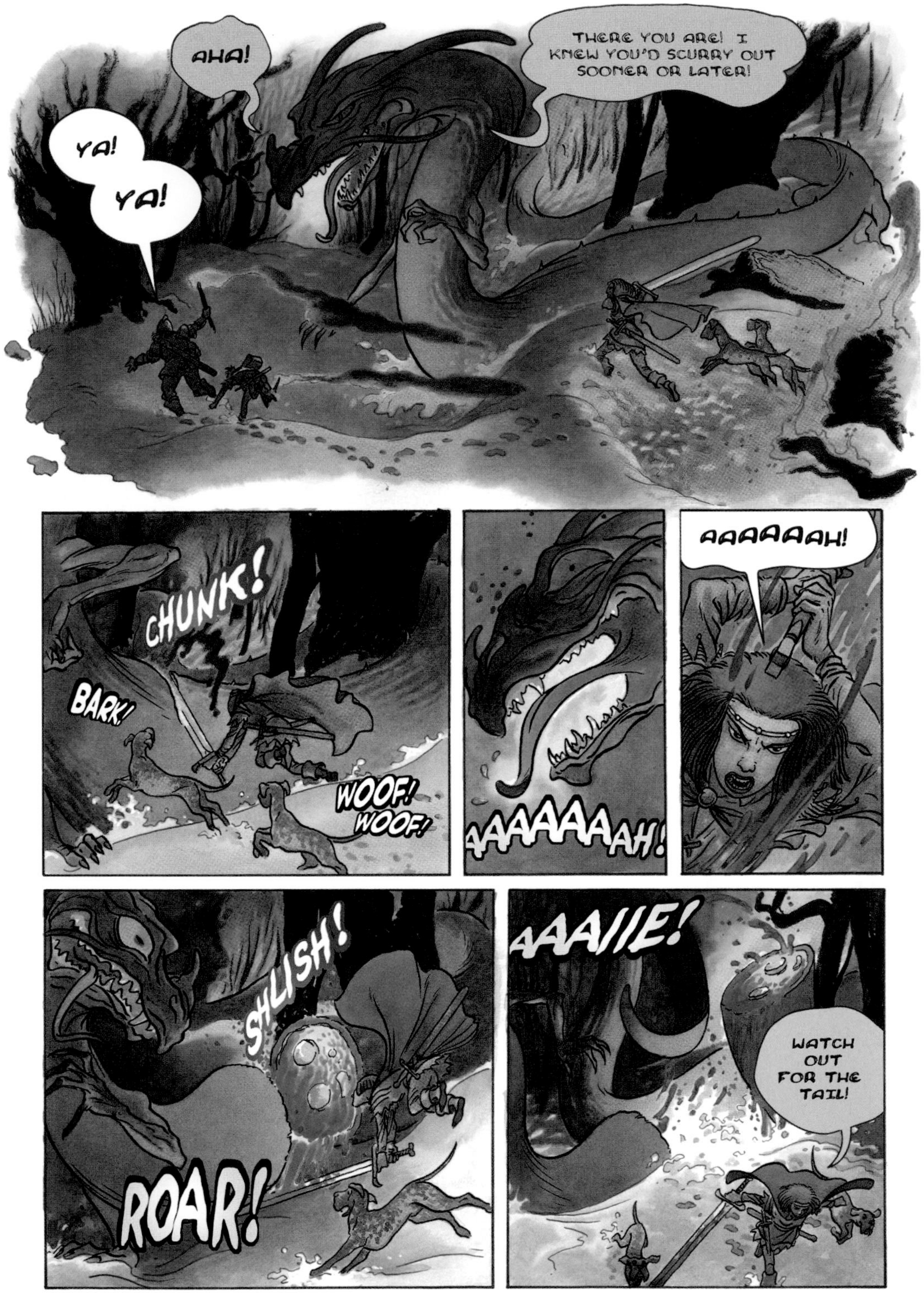
AHA!
THERE YOU ARE! I KNEW YOU'D SCURRY OUT SOONER OR LATER!
YA!
YA!
CHUNK!
BARK!
WOOF! WOOF!
AAAAAAAH!
AAAAAAH!
SHLISH!
ROAR!
AAAIIE!
WATCH OUT FOR THE TAIL!

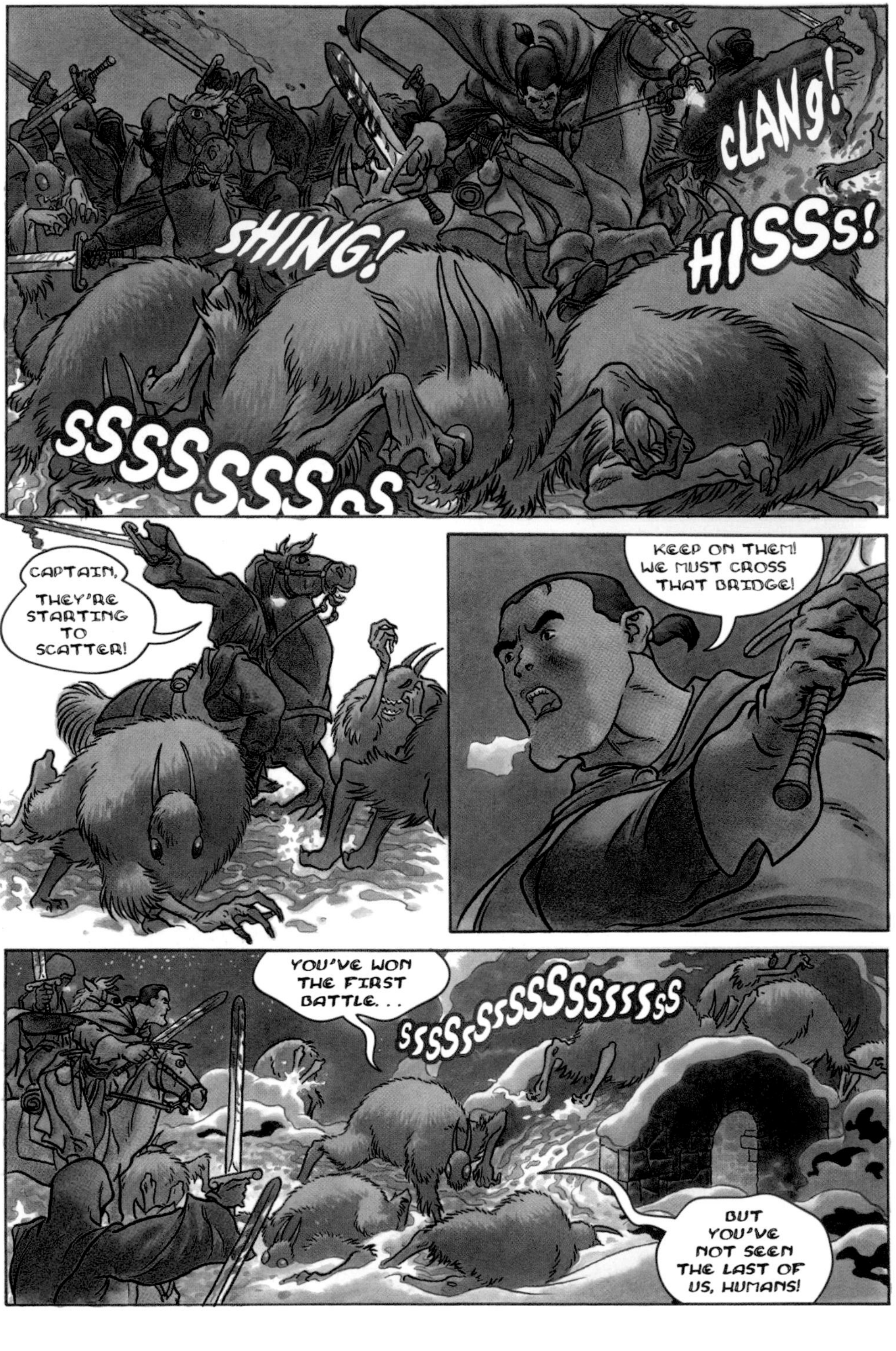

cLANG!
SHING!
HISSs!
SSSSSSSsS
CAPTAIN, THEY'RE STARTING TO SCATTER!
KEEP ON THEM! WE MUST CROSS THAT BRIDGE!
YOU'VE WON THE FIRST BATTLE. . .
SSSSsSsSSSSSSSSSsS
BUT YOU'VE NOT SEEN THE LAST OF US, HUMANS!

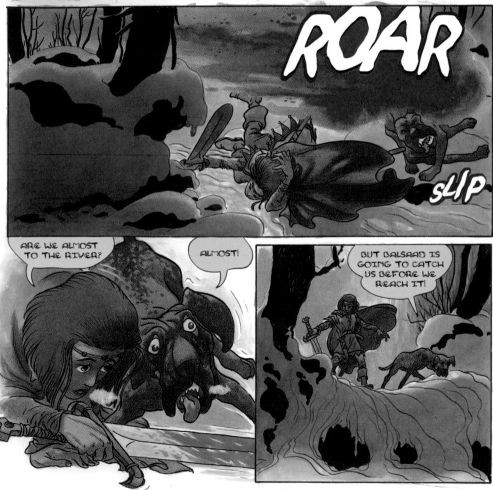

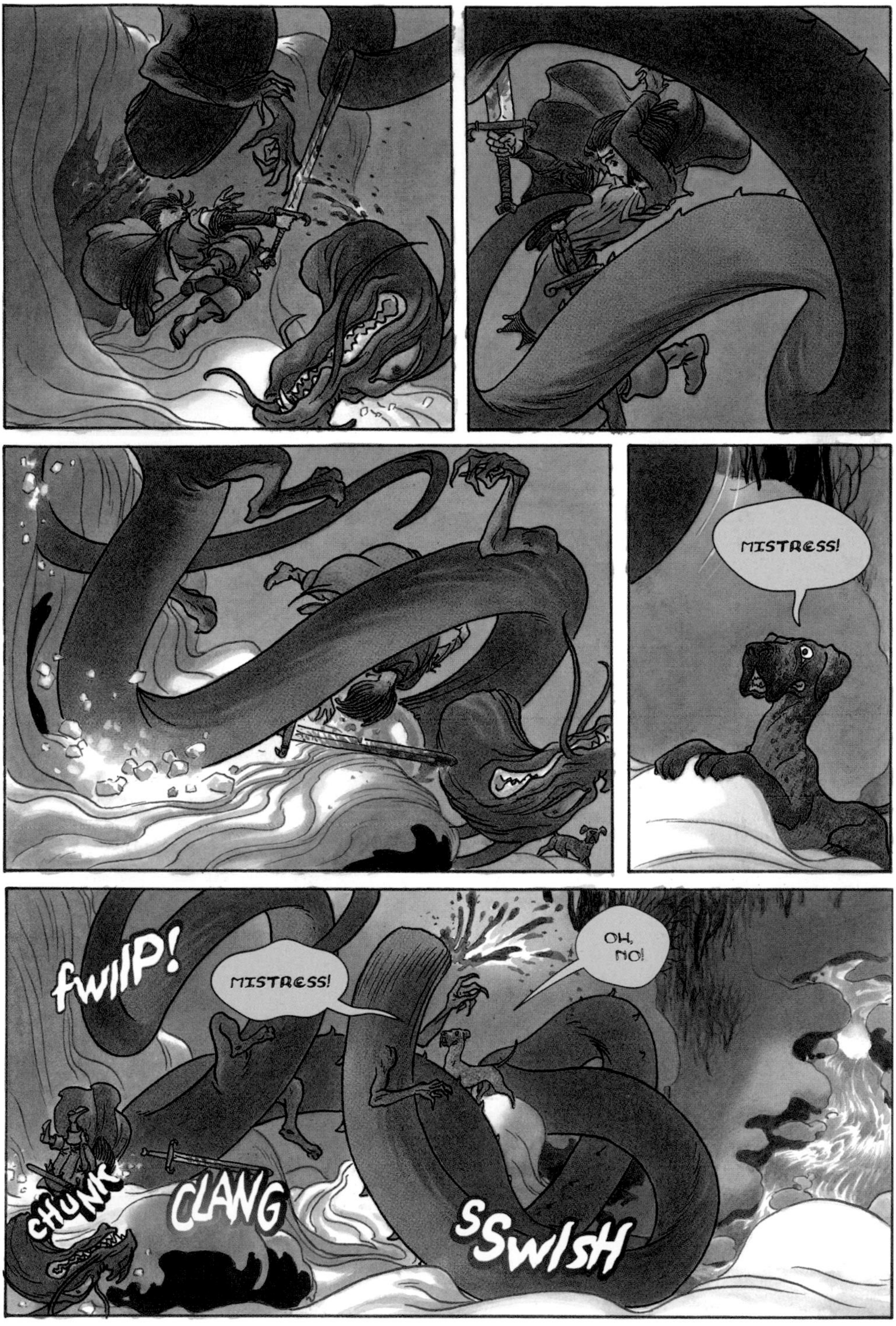
MISTRESS!
fwilP!
MISTRESS!
OH, NO!
CHUNK
CLANG
SSWISH

ROSE

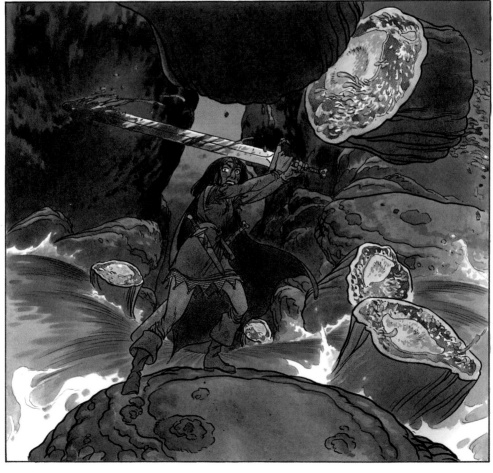

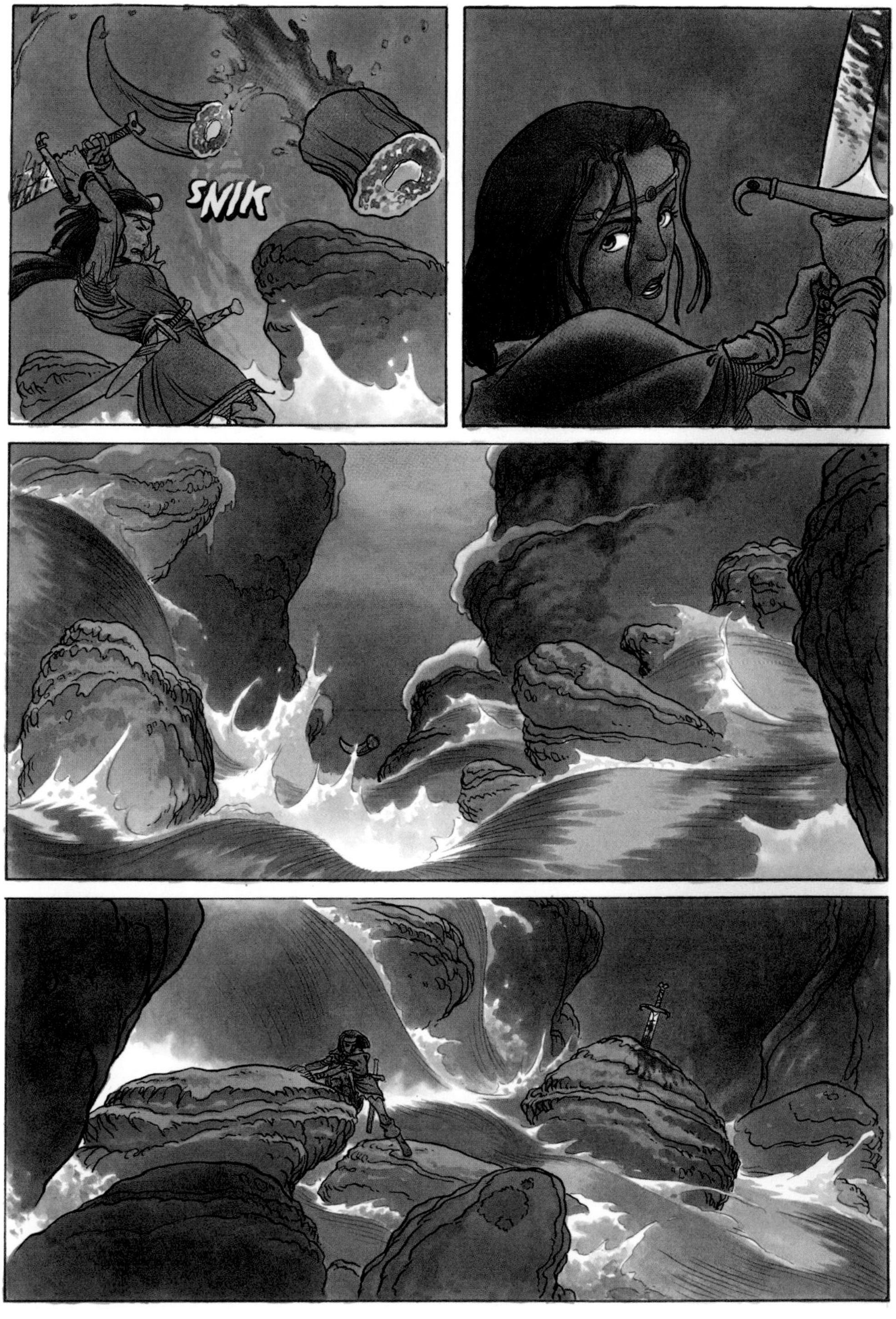
SNIK

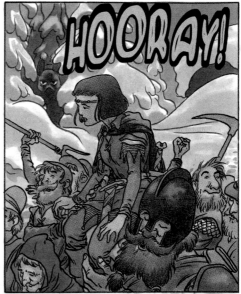

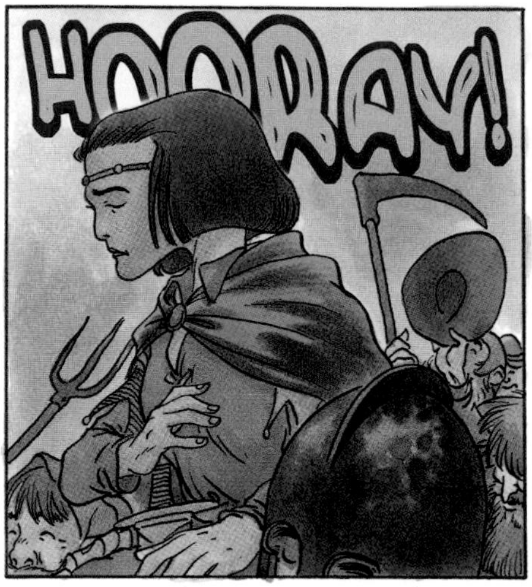
HOORAY!

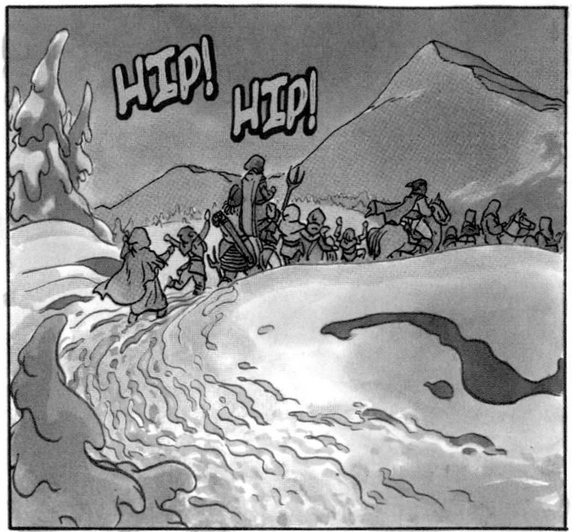
HIP!
HIP!

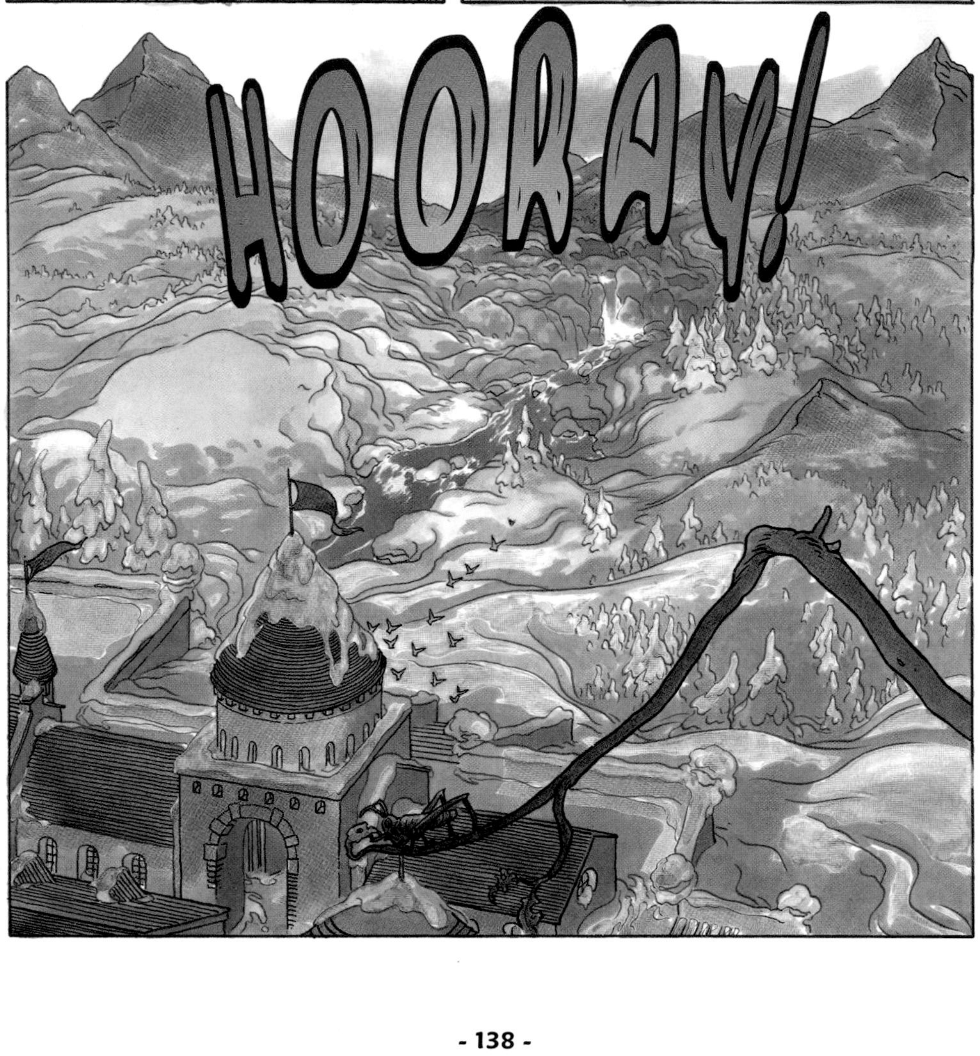
HOORAY!

THE END

About JEFF SMITH

JEFF SMITH was born and raised in the American Midwest and learned about cartooning from comic strips, comic books, and watching animated shorts on TV. After four years of drawing comic strips for The Ohio State University's student newspaper and co-founding Character Builders animation studio in 1986, Smith launched the comic book *BONE* in 1991. Between *BONE* and other comics projects, Smith spends much of his time on the international guest circuit promoting comics and the art of graphic novels. Visit him at www.boneville.com.

About CHARLES VESS

CHARLES VESS has published award-winning works with Marvel, DC, and Cartoon Books, and one of his two Eisner awards was for his paintings in *Rose*. Vess collaborated with Neil Gaiman on their book *Stardust* (now a movie on DVD), for which he won the World Fantasy Award for Best Artist in 1999. He also illustrated *Seven Wild Sisters*, written by Charles de Lint, and *The Green Man: Tales from the Mythic Forest*, both of which were American Library Association Best Books. The design and co-sculpting of a bronze fountain based on *A Midsummer Night's Dream* has kept him busy for the last two years. Vess lives on a small farm in Virginia, and you can visit him at www.greenmanpress.com.